Praise for the Danvers Novels

"Enough bittersweet longing to pluck your heartstrings and enough heat to keep it interesting."
—*Kirkus Reviews*

"Wonderful. . . . Landon's foray into contemporary romance has just the right amount of angst, sass, sexiness, humor, and, of course, romance."
—Fresh Fiction

"If you like the Cinderella-style story, this modern-day version is sure to be a hit."   —Once Upon a Twilight

Keeping It
Hot

THE BREAKFAST IN BED SERIES

SYDNEY LANDON

BERKLEY SENSATION
New York

BERKLEY SENSATION
Published by Berkley
An imprint of Penguin Random House LLC
375 Hudson Street, New York, New York 10014

ISBN: 9780399583223

First Edition: July 2017

Printed in the United States of America
1   3   5   7   9   10   8   6   4   2

Cover photo of pool by Tom Merton/Getty Images; photo of man by
Riccardo Piccinini/Shutterstock Images
Cover design by Colleen Reinhart
Book design by Laura K. Corless

Keeping It
Hot

One

Zoe Hart walked through the familiar lobby of the Oceanix Resort in Pensacola, Florida, but she saw none of its usual elegance and grandeur. She'd woken in a bad mood that morning, which was unusual since she normally loved her birthday. She was twenty-nine today, and despite her best attempts, she was no closer to seducing Dylan Jackson, her best friend and landlord, than she had been last year.

She owned and operated the coffee shop in the Oceanix, Zoe's Place. Even though she worked her ass off to make it a success, she was also grateful to Dylan for giving her a chance when she was trying to get her business off the ground. All the big coffee chains had vied to open a location in the ultra-high-end resort, but Dylan had believed in her business plan and had celebrated her success every step of the way.

Her close friend and shop manager, Dana Anders, was busy loading the pastry display cases for another busy breakfast rush when Zoe arrived. The comforting smell of freshly brewed coffee filled the air, and her stomach growled in response. For the first time that morning, she took a moment to appreciate her surroundings. She'd designed the interior layout with comfort in mind but had also wanted a place that appealed to a variety of customers. There were tables for her business customers who wanted to work while they drank their espressos, there were sofas for those who were truly enjoying their vacations and wanted to relax while they sipped frappes, and there were overstuffed chairs arranged in cozy seating areas for the groups who were recharging with a latte after a long day at the office or relishing a morning away from the kids. Of course, with their location inside the hotel, they had many customers who visited once and never returned, but she was particularly proud of the loyal local customers who had become like her friends and family.

"Well, well," Dana murmured as she noticed Zoe's dejected expression. "The birthday girl doesn't seem to be in the mood to celebrate this morning." Her friend patted the counter and sat down on a stool behind it. "Park it right there and tell me all about it."

Zoe shook her head in disgust. "I'm twenty-nine, still carrying around my big V-card, and I've been friend-zoned by the man I've secretly lusted after for years. So yeah, not exactly in the mood to celebrate another year of my love life going nowhere."

"Finally! I can't believe you're admitting this. I've been waiting forever for you to ask me for help. Whenever I brought it up, you always acted like you had no idea what I was talking about. Oh, and by the way, friend-zoned would be easier to deal with. Some friends have sex together all the time. You've been sister-zoned, and that's the kiss of death if you're hoping for a fling."

Zoe planted her hands on the counter and shook her head vehemently. "I haven't been sister-zoned. I'm still completely and totally in the friend area. Dylan and I are buddies. We talk about all kinds of things you wouldn't discuss with your sibling."

Dana clucked her tongue before taking a big drink of the coffee she had sitting nearby. Finally, as if she were talking to a toddler, she said, "Sweetie, when he hangs out with you, does he take calls and texts from other women?"

"Of course." Zoe ground her teeth, thinking of how much she hated overhearing him employing his sexy laugh on some bimbo of the month.

Putting a hand under her chin, Dana studied her for a moment before asking, "Does he ever tell you

3

anything about his dates? As in bedroom stuff or kink level?"

"Yes, all the time," Zoe growled. "I guess that proves that he doesn't see me as his sister, though, right?"

"It's worse than I thought," Dana said dramatically. "You're officially one of the guys. You've ceased to have a vagina where he's concerned."

"*What?* No way!" Zoe sputtered. Pointing to her ample chest, she argued, "How could he miss these babies?"

Refusing to back down, Dana fired off, "Does he ever bump you on the shoulder with his fist? Or high-five you?"

Zoe's mouth went dry and she stared at Dana in growing horror before dropping her head onto the counter. "Oh God, I'm just like one of his guy friends," Zoe mumbled in despair. "You're absolutely right. I might as well have a penis."

Dana patted the top of her head consolingly. "I don't know about the whole having-a-dick thing. I'd say you're more gender neutral where he's concerned."

"Wow, that's so much better," she snapped. Dana was silent for so long, Zoe finally lifted her head, thinking maybe they'd had a customer wander in before the shop officially opened. Instead, her friend was giving her a calculating look that immediately made her nervous. "What?" she asked warily, not even sure she wanted to know what was running through the other woman's mind. She and Dana were about as opposite as two people could be, but regardless of that, their friendship worked. Dana loved men in all shapes and sizes and seemed to be dating a new guy every week. She was adventurous, outgoing, and the customers absolutely adored her. She stood just over five feet tall with short blond hair and a personality that made everyone feel special. A few years back, not long after Zoe had hired her, Dana had convinced her to come out for a drink. Zoe had ended up having several past her limit and had drunkenly admitted to Dana that she'd had a crush on Dylan for years. She'd also confessed to being a virgin, something that had blown the other woman away. After that, Dana had tried her best to set Zoe up on blind dates, but none of them compared to the infatuation she carried where Dylan was concerned. The heart wanted what it wanted—and Zoe's appeared to be particularly stubborn.

Dana folded her arms and leaned forward. "You can come back from this. As long as you haven't entered the death zone where he looks at you like his little sister, there's always hope. We can turn this around . . . *if* you'll really apply yourself. Starting with that." Dana pointed to Zoe's white polo shirt as she spoke.

Zoe frowned, looking down in confusion. "What's wrong with my clothes?"

"Sweetie, if you want Dylan to stop seeing you as a

member of his dude squad, then you can't continue to dress like one of the guys." When Zoe opened her mouth to protest, Dana held her hand up. "What are they wearing when they come in here for coffee before hitting the golf course?"

"I've never noticed—" Zoe began before Dana interrupted her.

"Cut the crap," Dana huffed. "You know they dress just like that. Polo shirts and khaki shorts. Dylan sees you as one of the guys because you blend in so well with them. It's time for that to stop. You have so much going for you. Big tits, small waist, and plenty of butt. You need to dress to showcase your assets." As Zoe gulped, Dana pointed to her hair. "And that spinster ponytail has got to go. Your hair is gorgeous, but I've only seen you wear it down a few times and that was when I hid those freaking bands that you seem to have a million of. Men go crazy over long, wavy hair, which you naturally possess. You don't need a lot of makeup because you look great without it. Let's just start with the things that I've mentioned and I guarantee that Dylan will be tripping over his tongue in no time. Let me give you a makeover for your birthday. Whether you realize it or not, it'll help you with your self-confidence. And that is something that will benefit you in every aspect of your life. Getting the guy is just an added bonus."

"I don't know . . ." Zoe murmured. "Clothes really

don't change anything. I'm still the same person that he's known for years. I could probably parade around naked in front of him and it wouldn't make a difference. It seems silly to pretend to be someone I'm not."

Dana walked around the counter and put an arm around her. "Honey, men are visual creatures. You and Dylan have been friends since you were children. He's grown up thinking of you in a certain way. We're just attempting to show him that there is another side he's never seen before. He's overlooking the fact that you're a beautiful woman who is flipping perfect for him. Right or wrong, sometimes a new set of curtains makes the room look completely different."

A giggle burst from her lips and Zoe grinned at Dana. "Are you comparing me to draperies now?"

"Hey, I'm just trying to give you something to work with. Now go ahead and tell me you're on board. No, let's go one better than that." Dana pulled far enough away to extend a hand to her. "Zoe. Do you agree to do whatever it takes to finally land the man of your dreams this year? Are you prepared to surrender that V-card to Dylan before your thirtieth birthday? If so, let's shake on it. No wimping out, though. We're declaring war on the friend zone with Dylan. Are you ready to trade in your polos for plunging necklines and rising hemlines? Once you agree, there's no going back."

As Dana wiggled her hand impatiently, Zoe thought

back over the revelations her friend had just placed at her feet. Could it really be that simple? Had Dylan overlooked the fact that she was a potential romantic partner because she'd never made the effort to show off her femininity? And truthfully, she knew that she dressed for comfort most days. Her mother, who'd been the executive chef at the Oceanix for years, rarely wore makeup or fancy outfits, so Zoe hadn't grown up wearing dresses or bows in her hair. She'd been a tomboy and possibly she'd never stopped seeing herself that way.

But now she was almost thirty and she couldn't keep pining away for a man who didn't want her. She would let Dana help her and spend this next year giving it everything she had. If at the end she and Dylan were still only friends, then she'd have to accept that and move on with her life. As much as she cared for him, she wanted a husband and children of her own at some point in the future.

So, straightening her spine, Zoe took Dana's hand and gave it an enthusiastic shake. "Let's do this," she said bravely. *Please let Dylan be the one*, she thought to herself as she listened to Dana's plans for their first steps. The next twelve months might not go as Zoe wanted, but they certainly wouldn't be boring.

Two

It had been a hell of a long week and Dylan Jackson was looking forward to kicking back and relaxing. He usually had dinner with Zoe at least one evening a week, but thanks to a business trip to one of the other Oceanix Resorts, it had been closer to two weeks since he'd seen her last and he missed her. He'd even missed her birthday, which he tried never to do. He'd texted her earlier and she'd suggested they meet in one of the resort restaurants since neither of them had felt like cooking. Dylan lived in the penthouse, so it was a simple matter for him to take the elevator back down-stairs at seven. He'd figured Zoe was working late at the coffee shop as she usually did, but when she responded to his text, she'd already been at her condo a short distance from the hotel.

He walked into the restaurant and automatically headed for his usual reserved table in the corner. It was private and had an amazing view of the Gulf. He'd been so busy looking around that he was abruptly brought up short when he realized that his table was occupied. A woman with long, dark hair cascading down her back sat in one of the chairs sipping a glass of wine. Dylan stifled a surge of irritation. Even though the woman looked stunning from behind, now he'd have to deal with the aggravation of finding somewhere else to sit himself, which would be no small feat, as the restaurant was packed.

As he stood uncertainly pondering his options, the woman turned, seemingly sensing him behind her, and he froze. He blinked a few times, thinking he was imagining things. Then she smiled and it hit him with the force of a sledgehammer. "What are you waiting for, an engraved invitation?" She laughed as she motioned him closer.

Dear God, what is going on here? The woman with the short, clingy dress, amazing legs, and plump breasts sounded like his best friend. If he looked closely, her features were the same. But everything else was wrong—very wrong. Zoe wore her hair in a ponytail and dressed in sensible clothing. Half the time she had a coffee stain on her white polo. She didn't make his mouth go dry—or his cock go hard. She was his buddy, the one constant in his life that never changed.

"Did someone die?" he finally asked, thinking maybe she'd been to a funeral or something. Why else would she be wearing a dress?

She wrinkled her nose, as she was prone to do when she was thinking, before shaking her head. "Er . . . no." Giving him a look of concern, she reached out and put a hand on his arm. "Are you all right? You look pale. Would you rather we just go upstairs to your place and order in? I'm fine with that if you're tired."

"*No!*" he protested loudly, causing people at nearby tables to look over at him. Great, he was making an ass out of himself. But there was no way he was going somewhere more private with Zoe looking like . . . that. He needed to get to the bottom of this, preferably in public with lots of people around. So he took a breath and made an effort to collect himself. He stepped forward and took his seat. He was saved from making conversation while they placed their orders, but after the waiter had gone, an unusually awkward silence settled between them.

This type of thing never happened with them, and he found he wasn't sure how to handle it. Should he go ahead and ask her why she looked the way she did? Or ignore it and hope it never happened again?

She moved closer to him, putting her new and im-proved breasts only inches from his hand. "You seem a little stressed out," she said softly. "Are you sure you're okay?"

To his utter horror, he heard himself blurting out, "What's happened to you?" He pointed to her outfit, and then quickly gulped down a mouthful of his water. Maybe he was getting sick. His throat was so parched.

"What are you talking about?" she asked, looking at him as if he'd lost his mind. Hell, he was beginning to think she was right. He needed to check into his family's health history a little closer.

He knew he sounded nuts, but he couldn't stop himself from saying, "The dress, and the hair. You're even wearing high heels. You know those make your feet hurt."

"Oh, I've got a date later." Zoe shrugged. She gave him a bright smile, and then began filling him in on what he'd missed at the resort while he was away. She appeared to have no clue that he wasn't an active participant in the conversation. Making small talk seemed impossible for him right now; because all he wanted to do was demand to know who she was going out with. He figured they'd watch a movie after dinner as they normally did, but apparently that wasn't going to happen. Dylan had never been one for change, and this transformation was almost more than he could wrap his head around. He knew Zoe, though. This was just a one-time thing. She'd go back to looking the way she usually did tomorrow and then his world would be back in balance once again. Otherwise, he was going to have to face the fact that somewhere along the way his best friend had turned into a very desirable woman. And that, he was afraid, could only spell disaster for the relationship that he'd always valued above all others in his life.

⤴

Zoe had just arrived home when her phone began ringing. She pulled it from her purse and saw Dana's name on the screen. No doubt her friend had been going crazy wondering how dinner had gone with Dylan. Zoe clicked Answer, and with no preamble said, "Thanks to you, I'm home alone now when I could have spent a few hours with Dylan." Dana had insisted that Zoe say she had a date later on. According to the other woman, she was "too available" to her friend and needed to at least pretend to have a life outside of work and him. "Does 'all dressed up with nowhere to go' mean anything to you?"

Dana laughed for what seemed like five minutes. "Oh, come on, what did you really miss out on? Watching *Game of Thrones* while you lusted after him and he sat there, clueless as usual? Now stop whining and tell me what his reaction was at dinner. Please, God, he did actually notice you were dressed up, right? If he didn't, we need to investigate his sexual preferences further, because he'd have to be batting for the other team not to appreciate how hot you look tonight."

Zoe flopped down on her sofa and cradled the phone between her shoulder and ear as she reflected back on the evening. Finally, she admitted, "He was rattled and it might have been because of me. He wanted to know why I was wearing a dress. He asked if someone had died." When Dana's laughter quieted, Zoe added uncertainly, "But I don't think he was feeling well. His face was red and he was sweating—a lot. So I'm not sure how much credit I can take for his unusual behavior. He'd chewed almost a whole pack of antacid tablets by the time dinner was finished."

"I'm betting he was feeling just dandy before the new and improved Zoe blew his little world apart," she giggled.

Frowning, Zoe asked, "So we're happy that I might have driven him to sickness tonight?"

"Hell yeah," Dana crowed. "That's called pushing Dylan right out of the shallow end and into shark-infested waters. You're his safety net and you have been for years. He knows he can always count on good ole dependable Zoe when he wants to chill with a buddy. He never even considers the fact for one moment that you might have a life or, God forbid, plans of your own. No, he figures he can drop in on you without a moment's notice and you'll be there in your flannel pants and sloppy T-shirt to entertain him. That shit needs to stop now. If he wants your time, then he has to make plans with you in advance, because your social calendar is booking up fast."

"It is?" Zoe asked uncertainly. "Oh, wait . . . You mean my imaginary one. I'm not sure how long I can pull that off. Won't he actually need to see me with someone a few times to make it look convincing? Maybe I can ask my cousin from Georgia to play along."

"You're going out with Mike's friend tomorrow night. I've already made all the arrangements. Now we just need to figure out a way for Dylan to see you with him."

Cringing, Zoe asked, "M-Mike as in the guy you've been dating, like, a week? Do you really think that's a good idea? You couldn't possibly know anything about him."

"You remember Paul, right? We went out for a few months. He owns the gym in town."

Having no idea where this was going, Zoe said, "Sure, the one with the big . . . biceps." He'd come in the coffee shop a few times to pick Dana up. Zoe had never heard him say anything other than "S'up," but she tried not to judge.

"Yep, that's him. Anyway, that's Mike's friend. I dated Paul first, but we broke up when I met Mike. You don't need to worry, though, there were no hard feelings and we're all still friends."

"But . . . he's your ex-boyfriend," Zoe sputtered. "I

can't go out with him! That's breaking all kinds of sister codes."

"Zoe, we weren't married or anything. And I have no plans to hook up with him again." Dana's voice lowered to not much above a whisper as she added, "To be such a big guy everywhere else, his dick was a tad on the petite side. Plus, with all the steroids he was doing, it took far too much effort on my part to get that little thing to a full salute, if you know what I mean."

Zoe shook her head before dropping it back onto the sofa. "So let me get this straight. You're setting me up with a man with a small pecker who can't get it up? Geez, I'd hate to think what you'd do to someone you didn't like."

Dana giggled before saying, "It's brilliant. We both know you're not going to sleep with him, and he's not likely to put as much pressure on you to hook up since there's nothing much going on under his hood. I figure you two can do something safe like go to a movie. That way the conversation will be limited. And we'll somehow arrange for an accidental sighting by Dylan. Perfect, right?"

"I guess," Zoe grudgingly admitted. "Are you sure he's not going to expect *that* from me?"

"Oh, no way," Dana assured her. "For a little added insurance, I told him you were gay and had just recently been dumped by your girlfriend. He was sympathetic when I mentioned what a hard time you were having with the breakup."

"Wait—what?" Zoe screeched out as she sat up abruptly. "He thinks I'm gay?"

"Did you want him hitting on your virgin ass?" Dana countered.

"Good point," Zoe sighed. "God, I can't believe I'm going along with this. And I have no idea how we'll accidentally run into Dylan. Without that happening, this whole date is kind of pointless, isn't it?"

Zoe could practically hear Dana rubbing her hands together when she said, "Leave that part to me. We'll work out all the details tomorrow and plan your outfit. I'm thinking you need to go with another dress since Dylan responded so well to the one you wore tonight."

Shaking her head, Zoe said sarcastically, "Really? He almost broke out into hives and he had huge armpit stains from all the sweating. I'm not certain we can consider that a positive reaction. Wouldn't something like a heart attack have been better?"

Sounding absolutely serious, Dana said, "Of course it would have, but we've got to work up to that. Now go get your beauty sleep, and whatever you do, don't answer any calls or texts from Dylan tonight. He might decide to check up on you to see if you're already home or so bored on your date that you'd use your phone."

Those words had barely left Dana's lips when Zoe's phone chimed with an incoming text.

Dylan: So, how's the date going so far?

"Who's texting you?" Dana demanded, apparently having heard.

"Er . . . it's Dylan wanting to know how my date is going. I could just send a quick one back saying fine. I don't want him to be worried about me when I don't respond."

"*No!*" Dana snapped. "Don't you dare reply to that until the morning. That way he'll spend the rest of the night wondering if you're doing the nasty with some other guy while he's sitting home alone."

"But—" Zoe started to protest before Dana cut her off.

"How many nights have you sat home while he's been out with some other woman? Aren't you finally ready to be the one with the power here? He's had the best of both worlds for far too long and that shit stops tonight. You're the new and improved Zoe now. You're a social butterfly and he's damn well going to need to know that your world no longer revolves around him. Can I get an amen?"

"Amen?" Zoe muttered, knowing it sounded more like a question than a shout of girl power.

"Leave your phone in the kitchen and go to bed . . . now," Dana instructed. "Because if you stay up any later, you'll be tempted to text him back. And if you do . . . I'll know," the other woman threatened.

Zoe thought longingly of the text awaiting a response and gulped. "All right, I promise I won't text him back. I'll see you at the shop tomorrow. You're working the evening shift, right?"

"Yep, I'll see you around four. That should give us plenty of time to get you squared away for your date."

After they ended the call, she stood, and holding her phone as if it were a snake, she ran to the kitchen and set it on the counter before heading to her bedroom. For good measure, she closed and locked her door as if the damn phone had legs and would break in somehow. She'd never ignored Dylan before and she knew that it was going to be a long night. Somehow doing what was necessary to get his attention seemed a heck of a lot harder than spending the evening with her best friend. She had to believe it would all be worth it in the end, though, when he finally saw her as a woman and not just as one of the guys.

Dylan looked down at his phone once again, thinking that possibly he hadn't heard the text chime when he was in the kitchen. But no, there was still nothing. If it had been a regular landline, he would have already resorted to checking the damn thing for a dial tone. Since when had Zoe ever ignored a text from him? It had been a fucking hour. More than enough time to reply. Oh shit, did she even know the guy she was going out with tonight? Maybe he should call her, just to make sure everything was okay.

Don't do it, man, his subconscious screamed. She had the right to a social life. How many times had he gotten some form of communication from her while he was with a woman? Did he drop everything and respond right away? No, more often than not, he silenced his phone and got back to the business at hand. Then he called Zoe on the way home, or if it was too late, he'd check in the next morning unless it had been something that needed to be addressed that evening. So going by his own behavior, wasn't it reasonable for her to also follow that same protocol when out with another man? *But my Zoe doesn't date.* And that's what was bugging him more than he cared to admit. She'd blown him off after dinner and that shit just didn't happen. Since they were kids, he'd always come first with her. She was the one he could count on to catch a last-minute movie or have a lazy night at home with. They'd stuff themselves with pizza and watch whatever television show they were obsessed with at the moment. She'd come over in her ratty pajamas with her hair in a sloppy ponytail and they'd each take over a corner of his couch until one or both of them fell asleep. He'd woken countless times to find that it was already morning and Zoe was snoring away with her mouth hanging open.

He'd fully expected for that to happen tonight as well, but then, he'd been seriously freaked out at dinner when he met the Zoe2017. That's what he'd come to think of her transformation as. For some reason she'd picked this year to change almost overnight, and dammit, he didn't like it. All right, possibly he was intrigued by this new . . . chesty version, but it felt so wrong. He didn't stare at his best friend's tits, even if they were so perky that he'd practically had to sit on his hands to keep from reaching out to touch them. And that ass . . . Mother of God! When she'd bent to get her napkin, which had fallen to the floor, he'd literally drooled right there.

Then, as they were leaving the restaurant, he'd discovered something even more horrifying—those high-heeled shoes she was wearing made those perfect tits bounce in an alarming way. Was she even wearing a bra? He'd been so rattled by then that he'd had a hard time walking. He was equal parts appalled and intrigued. Of course, he was also a guy and couldn't figure out what he wanted to stare at more, her tits, ass, or legs. Then there was the internal conflict as he tried to remind himself that she was just like a sister to him. It had been a hell of a lot easier to accept that when she hadn't been so freaking hot. Where were her damn khakis and polo?

When his phone rang, he nearly jumped out of his skin. He fumbled trying to answer the call. "Zoe," he said without bothering to look at the ID.

"Not the last time I checked," replied an amused voice that was definitely not Zoe's.

Releasing a heavy sigh, Dylan asked, "What can I do for you, Ash?" His brother Asher ran the Oceanix resort in Charleston and was a frequent visitor to Florida. Dylan was both blessed and cursed to be close to all of his brothers. Each of them ran one of the resorts. Rhett ran the Miami location, then there was Luke, who handled one of their new resorts in St. Croix. Their uncle Judson and cousins Alex, Leo, Erik, and Lila ran the remaining resorts.

"Has sweet Zoe flown the coop tonight? Not a lovers' tiff, I hope?" His brothers had teased him for years about his friendship with Zoe. None of them could fathom how he could have a platonic relationship with a woman. He'd assured them that he'd never even come close to having sex with her, which had downright shocked them. The first time Ash had met her, he'd announced that she had potential, but needed to sex things up a bit. Dylan could only imagine what the other man would say if he'd gotten a look at her tonight. *Note to self, keep them away from each other if her strange behavior continues.*

Hoping to keep the explanation brief and change the subject, Dylan said vaguely, "Er . . . no, I had just texted her earlier and figured it was her. No big deal. So what's up?" Shit, had his voice risen higher for the last part of that statement?

Asher as usual seemed to know when he was trying to avoid talking about something and kept right on going. "I thought she dropped everything for you. You seem a little jumpy. Has something happened?"

Before he knew it, Dylan was pouring out exactly what had occurred at dinner. It was the last thing he should have done but he desperately needed to vent to someone. Normally, that would be Zoe . . . but he couldn't very well tell her how much she'd thrown him. "I mean, I didn't know it was possible for her to look like that. There's a woman's body under that usual coffee shop uniform she wears."

Asher laughed hysterically before he finally got it together enough to say, "You both work at a hotel right on the beach. Don't tell me you've never seen her in a swimsuit before. This shouldn't have been a total shock to you."

"Well, of course I have, but it was some kind of one-piece number with a skirt on it."

He could almost hear Ash wincing as he said, "Fuck, I hate those things. I don't care what size a woman is, she should just own it. Don't go out there wearing a damn sheet tied around your waist. If you have a big butt, put that sucker out there. Lots of men like some extra junk in the trunk. What they don't like is seeing you wearing your gown on the beach. You should have staged an intervention with her long ago. Friends don't let friends dress like that."

Dylan shrugged his shoulders, not getting what the big deal was. "I think she looked fine. Plus, she didn't need as much sunscreen. Some of those skimpy suits are just skin cancer waiting to happen. Zoe was very sensible to choose the suits that she did."

"Dude, do you even hear yourself?" Ash asked incredulously. "If I hadn't seen you pick up a lot of women in my time, I'd have to seriously question your manhood right now. 'Sensible'? Who in the hell cares about that? One of the great things about our jobs is the endless parade of half-naked women that walk through the doors every day. Please tell me you aren't down there handing out SPF50 and sun hats to them. I mean, I know you're working in the retirement capital of the United States, but there are some women there under seventy, right?"

"Screw you," Dylan snapped. "I'm talking about Zoe, not other women. She's my best friend and I'm happy she watches after herself like that."

"Ah, I see," Ash said smugly. "You just want her covered up so neither you nor any other guy will look at her twice. That way she can remain at your beck and call and there's no muddying of the waters because it keeps things nice and safe with your buddy. That about cover it?"

"Wh-what? No," Dylan sputtered. "That's not it at all. She's free to have a life and dress in any way that she chooses. She's always been more on the conservative side and I think it suits her personality."

"Holy shit," Ash groaned out. "Bro, if you can't be honest with me, then at least don't lie to yourself. That shit gets painful after a while. You've had Zoe in a box all these years. I'll admit, we may not understand it, but I think all of us have envied what you've got going on with her. We've also wondered why it's never gone beyond friendship. Outside of whatever woman you're casually seeing, Zoe is your significant other and always has been. You're practically like one of the suburban couples who finish each other's sentences. Heck, I would have figured by now you'd have married her and there'd be some baby Jacksons running around there."

"You've lost your mind." Dylan laughed. "I've told you time and again, there is nothing like that between me and her. Never even been tempted."

"Sounds like you were tonight," Ash interjected. "What are you planning to do if this wasn't just a one-time thing? If she had you that worked up during the hour it probably took for dinner, how will you deal if this is the norm from now on?"

Dylan sat quietly for a moment pondering his brother's words before he finally admitted, "It . . . I don't know. I'm afraid it would be a game changer and I don't think I want that. Zoe is my constant, the one thing in my life I can depend on that never changes. I'm not ready to let that go."

"That's your choice," Ash said, "but realize that you sitting at home wondering where she is may be your new reality. Nothing stays the same forever. We either adapt and move forward or we get left behind."

Pinching the bridge of his nose, Dylan said quietly, "Yeah, thanks for that. Listen, it's been a long day and I'm going to crash. I'll catch up with you tomorrow."

"No problem. But whatever you do, don't call or text her again tonight. You've already made one attempt and that's all any self-respecting man should do. Put your phone somewhere out of sight and go to bed."

Dylan clenched his teeth in frustration, because he had been planning to send just one more text in case she hadn't gotten the first tone. "Whatever," he grumbled, then ended the call. Before temptation got the best of him, he took the phone and set it on the kitchen counter. If there was any type of emergency with the resort, they had the number to his landline. Then he turned on his heel and practically ran for the bedroom. Damn, this was going to be one long night. *Why hasn't she contacted me?*

Three

Zoe had just opened the coffee shop the next morning when Dylan came striding through the doors. His hair was standing on end as if he'd run his hand through it countless times already and it was barely six. "Hey, buddy," she chirped as he took a seat at the bar. Unlike him, she'd always been a morning person. "You're looking a little rough. Anything happen?"

"I'm glad to see you're still alive," he snapped, then quickly averted his gaze to the menu boards behind her.

What is going on with him? "Um . . . did you think I wouldn't be?" she asked hesitantly as she tried to decipher his strange mood.

Still refusing to make eye contact, he tapped a finger

against the granite surface. "Well, I wasn't sure since you didn't bother replying to my text last night."

Ugh, this is bad. What do I say? Damn you, Dana! She attempted a casual laugh that came out more like nails on a chalkboard before saying, "I didn't hear it come through and it was so late by the time I got home. I knew you were probably already asleep by then and I didn't want to wake you."

Finally, he stopped his perusal of the menu board and looked at her for the first time. She saw his eyes widen as he took in the off-the-shoulder peasant top and jean shorts she was wearing. She'd almost chickened out this morning when she'd put them on, but after checking every angle in the mirror, she had to admit her outfit was more than flattering. She'd put her hair back in the usual work ponytail, but had added some hoop earrings to soften the style. All in all, she looked Florida casual, which was perfect for a coffee shop on the beach—even in an upscale hotel. *Is he . . . looking at my breasts?* No sooner had that thought entered her mind than she noticed his cheeks coloring as if guilty of that very thing. He cleared his throat loudly before saying, "I'll um . . . just have an espresso and a blueberry muffin." *Okay, so now we're changing the subject—interesting.*

"Sure," she replied easily as she turned to make his coffee. When she reached up to get a lid for his cup, she heard a harsh indrawn breath and glanced back questioningly. "Everything all right?"

Waving a hand at her, he asked, "So what's with the new clothes again? I know you said the dress last night was for a date, but you're all . . . different today. I thought that was a one-time thing."

Wow, someone is grumpy today. Zoe shrugged her shoulders as she put a cup in front of him. "Dana and I went shopping a few days ago. I guess I was in a bit of a wardrobe rut and she helped me pick out some new outfits." Deciding to test the waters, she twirled around once, giving her hips an extra shake. "Don't you like it? Apparently my usual work attire was a bit too boring. Dana said this was a fun look so I decided to give it a try."

Dylan looked her up and down for what seemed like forever. *Is he sweating again?* Zoe could see a light sheen on his forehead and she moved forward, leaning across the bar and laying her hand against his skin to check for a fever. He jerked as if shocked. "Wh-what are you doing?" he asked hoarsely.

"You're all flushed like you were last night. Maybe you've picked up a bug. Do you have a headache or does anything hurt? How about your stomach? Oh my God, even your eyes are glazed," she said in concern. "Why don't I call Dr. Fisher and see if he's available to drop by this morning?" Dr. Fisher had a family practice a few miles away, but also made emergency trips to the hotel if they had a guest who became ill.

Dylan gently pushed the hand that was still hovering in front of his face away. "Zoe, I'm fine. I walked the hotel grounds to look at the new landscaping before I came in here. It's already humid outside today and the suit I'm wearing isn't exactly cool. I assure you that I'm just dandy."

"But you were the same way at dinner last night," she pointed out uncertainly. "You know you should always get anything new checked out."

"It was hot last night as well, right? There's nothing more to it than that." He dropped his gaze and once again Zoe thought there was a strong possibility that he was looking at her boobs. Grabbing a towel from beside her, she decided to test her theory. Her breasts jiggled as she wiped at an imaginary smudge in front of him on the granite. She was elated to see his attention centered on her cleavage as it jiggled with her movements. Dana obviously knew what she was doing, because that was the only time other than last night in all the years of their friendship that Zoe had ever caught him checking her out. Wow, it was official: her old wardrobe was a man repellant. No wonder she'd easily been able to remain a virgin until the ripe old age of twenty-nine. She couldn't help thinking that the new padded bra was a big help as well. Wait, was that false advertising? Some poor guy thought you had big boobs, then discovered that under that Miracle Bra, you were a tad on the small side?

Knowing by his stubborn expression that he wouldn't change his mind, she said, "Well, if you're sure." She handed him his muffin and smiled as he took a big bite. The man had always been a slave to baked goods and that had never changed. If he wasn't so active, he'd probably be sporting some love handles by now. But his regular runs on the beach along with time in the resort gym kept his body hard and ripped. Now it was her staring at his chest as she pictured it without all the clothes he was currently wearing. Covertly watching him in a pair of swim trunks was one of her favorite pastimes. *Yes, folks, I'm nothing but an ogling pervert when he's around.* "So what's got you out and about so early this morning?"

Dylan pulled a napkin from a nearby dispenser and wiped his mouth. "I have a meeting with Margot Holder from the Chamber of Commerce about some upcoming events and—"

"Handsy Holder?" Zoe started laughing, remembering the fifty-something-year-old cougar who never missed an opportunity to hit on Dylan. She had hair like Dolly Parton and a body that seemed at odds with her age. Zoe was certain there had been some surgical enhancements there. And those fingernails? They were so long that she had no idea how the woman was able to function with them from day to day.

"I'm glad you find it so amusing"—he smirked—"because she's supposed to be here at seven."

Making a walking motion with her hands, Zoe said, "Well, you better run along and get prepared. Don't forget protection. Wait, she might be in menopause so that could be an added bonus, right?"

Shaking his head with a grin, Dylan asked, "Are you about done? Because if you are, I wanted to let you know that I'll be meeting her here. I'm glad you opened this morning because I know how much you two admire each other. Maybe when one of the other girls comes in, you can sit and chat for a while."

"What?" Zoe hissed. "No! You know she hates me. Why can't you use your office?"

Dylan propped his forearms on the counter and clucked his tongue. "Now, now, I'm sure that's not true. You've only met a handful of times. I seem to remember her complimenting your dress at the company Christmas party last year."

Putting her hands on her hips, Zoe grumbled, "I don't think 'Kmart has so many interesting choices these days, Moe' exactly counts as a compliment. Come on—how many women are named Moe? She does that on purpose."

Dylan chuckled, shaking his head. "I'd forgotten about that. I do remember her asking you at the barbecue if you were drinking Diet Coke. I thought you'd beat her into the ground with your glass that night."

"The woman's pure evil," Zoe huffed. "She has it in for me because she thinks I'm some sort of competition for you."

And just like that, things were weird again. Dylan shifted and avoided eye contact as he stared at the damn coffee board. Finally, he cleared his throat, seeming to realize that she was waiting for a response. "Um . . . yeah, she's obviously delusional." Getting abruptly to his feet, he pointed to a table near the wall. "I'm going to get settled over there. I need to return a few e-mails while I'm waiting. Go ahead and run a tab. I'm sure I'll need more coffee and Margot will probably want something."

"Sure, no problem," Zoe replied, wondering what she'd said to get to him this time. They'd always joked around with each other, and everything had been fine until she'd mentioned the competition thing. *Maybe he's getting the male version of PMS in his old age.*

Zoe pushed it out of her mind and busied herself filling the bakery cases. Her mother did most of the baking for the shop as a side job, and she'd used her key as she did every morning to drop some fresh items by on her way into work in the main dining room. A few minutes later, her morning baristas, Jill and Meg, walked in and Zoe spent a few moments with them going over the day before the first morning rush got under way. Out of the corner of her eye, she saw Margot Holder walk in the door and make a beeline for

Dylan. Her blond hair was expertly teased and sprayed into place. She was wearing a skintight dress that looked like something a teenager would wear and she was currently plastered all over Dylan in what Zoe could only think was her version of "good morning."

When his eyes met hers over the other woman's head, Zoe sighed in resignation. Dammit, she couldn't resist an unspoken plea for help and he was clearly giving her one. Moving around the counter as if going to her own execution, Zoe made her way slowly to their table, putting on her best fake smile. "Good morning, *Mrs.* Holder. How nice to see you again." Zoe could tell by the twitch of Dylan's lips that he'd caught her emphasis on the "Mrs." part.

At first, Margot gave her a blank look and Zoe figured the other woman was going to snub her and pretend not to recognize her. But then a smile curled those unnaturally plump lips and she purred, "Oh, hello there, Moe. I forgot that you worked here. Do you have any menus we can look at?"

"Zoe actually owns the place," Dylan pointed out.

"How nice for you," Margot said in a condescending voice. Turning back to Dylan, she added, "Wasn't I telling you the last time we were together how easy it is to start your own business now? Why, look, Moe is a perfect example of that."

Even Dylan was at a loss for words now. But Zoe was used to dealing with difficult customers, and right now, that's what Margot was. So taking a deep breath, Zoe asked, "So what can I get you? Dylan, would you like another espresso?" He nodded his head gratefully.

Margot reached out and put one of her long fingernails on the bottom of Zoe's shirt. "Do you not wear uniforms here? I think it's so important to maintain a professional demeanor." Wrinkling her nose, she added, "After all, if you give employees the leeway to dress as they'd like, then where does it end?" Margot turned her back, dismissing her without words and Zoe stood behind her clenching her hands. Normally, she could laugh off the veiled insults, but the other woman was being particularly nasty today and she wasn't sure how much more she could take. She put her hands near Margot's neck as if she was going to strangle her and she saw Dylan's eyes go wide. "I'll have a nonfat latte," Margot tossed over her shoulder, luckily without looking back.

"Sure," Zoe murmured sweetly. Stalking away, she returned to the counter and waited while Meg fixed their drinks. She was tempted to stir Margot's with her finger, but managed to refrain. Instead, she returned with the order. She handed Dylan his first, then put Margot's in front of her.

"This is nonfat, isn't it, Moe?" Margot asked in her faux friendly voice.

"It sure is," Zoe chimed. "After all, us girls have to watch the carbs when we get some age on us, don't we?" Dylan coughed, sounding as if he was strangling on his espresso, while Margot glared daggers at her. "If you need anything else, let me know." Not waiting around for a counterattack, Zoe turned and almost ran back to the sanctuary of the bar. She couldn't believe it was barely past seven in the morning and she'd already caught Dylan checking out her boobs and made a mortal enemy out of Handsy Holder. How could this day possibly get any better?

Dylan wanted to throttle Margot. What an absolute bitch. If he hadn't been sitting at the table attempting to pretend he wasn't staring at Zoe's incredible body in another new outfit, he would have told the woman off. Margot was an important mover and shaker in their town, but she'd crossed the line today. She'd moved from her usual catty comments to being downright mean. He had no idea why men got a bad rap for being hotheads, because women were fucking brutal. Hell, he'd rather take a fist to the gut straight up than be on the receiving end of all that psychological bullshit that the opposite sex loved so well. Although he had to admit that Zoe had certainly fired the last shot with that comment about the carbs. He'd damn near spit his coffee all over the table.

He was pretty sure that Margot knew she'd gone too far as well, because he'd barely been civil to her for the rest of their meeting. When they'd left, he hadn't seen Zoe behind the counter, and like the sap he was becoming, he missed her. He'd been in his office for a few hours now and had gotten absolutely nothing done. His feet were propped on his desk, for God's sake. But those tits, where in the ever-loving hell had they come from? Was there ever a good time to notice that your best friend was hot as fuck? He'd been horrified to realize that he had gotten hard when she'd bent over the counter to feel his forehead. An innocent gesture that had him thinking of stripping those shorts off her and burying himself balls deep in an attempt to fuck this confusion out.

A brief knock at the door had him dropping his feet abruptly. He might be the boss, but he still hated to be caught goofing off. He certainly wasn't setting much of an example today. His assistant, Lisa, stepped in and took in the situation with one glance. "I'm going to go ahead and admit that Zoe told me to let her know if you looked sick today. Apparently, you've been acting strange." Walking closer, she took a look at his computer and grinned. "Now I can report back that you're lazy and like to play Angry Birds when you're supposed to be working."

Dylan gave her a sheepish look. Lisa Merck had been with him for close to five years now, and they had a very informal relationship. She was spunky and irreverent, which meant they got along great. And unlike most of his other employees, she didn't care that he was a Jackson. She was also loyal, dedicated, and worked any and all hours necessary to help him ensure that the Oceanix ran smoothly. Luckily for him, her husband was an airline pilot and worked a lot of long hours, so she was happy to fill the time while he was away. Dylan always made sure that, if at all possible, she had some time off when her husband was at home. And they were free to make use of anything at the resort for free whenever they liked. He believed in rewarding his people, and Lisa was invaluable to him. "I was just gathering my thoughts," he said as he ended the game. It wasn't as if he'd actually been focusing on it anyway.

Lisa began straightening papers on his desk, which was a bit strange since she rarely touched them unless he asked her to help him find something. She was fond of saying that she wasn't his maid. "So . . . Zoe's made some changes."

He'd been so focused on her unusual behavior that he almost missed the words. "Um . . . what do you mean?" *That's it. When all else fails, act ignorant. It works every time.*

She gave up all pretense of organizing. "Oh, come on, Dylan, there's no way you missed that. She looks amazing. I mean, she's always been pretty, but in a very understated way. Now it's there for the whole world to see. And from the attention she was getting when I dropped by earlier, everyone is certainly noticing."

"Who was looking at her?" he snapped, then winced when she gave him a triumphant look. *Damn, I walked right into that one. Time for some damage control.* "Meaning I hope no one was bothering her. Some of the guests can be overly friendly, but she can handle herself."

Lisa crossed her arms and leaned a hip on the corner of his desk. "So, is that officially what you're going with?" When he shrugged as if to say no big deal, she pursed her lips for a moment and he thought the subject was closed. "Well . . . I guess it won't bother you then when I say that Dana told me Zoe has a big date tonight with someone she really likes. He's picking her up at the shop around seven." Dylan knew his mouth was hanging open, but he was helpless to control his reaction. Lisa made a big show of brushing her hands off and walking toward the door. "Oh, and it wasn't only the guests who were taking stock of Zoe's appearance. Mason was also down there drinking enough coffee to keep him awake for the next week."

"My operations manager?" Dylan asked incredulously. "What was he doing there? Don't I pay him to actually manage stuff around here?"

In a voice full of laughter, Lisa said, "Oh, I think he was doing his best to keep sight of your interests. You better make sure those Christmas bonuses are generous this year because most of your male employees are going to go broke drinking Zoe's coffee." With that parting shot, she was gone and he was left to fume in private.

Why was Zoe doing this to him? He'd left on a business trip and come home to find the world as he knew it all out of whack. Everyone at the hotel was on some kind of caffeine high, and he was just plain confused as to what he was feeling. And she had another date? She just went out last night, for God's sake. Plus, this one was supposedly special? Well, he'd see about that. He planned to be sitting down there in the coffee shop when Mr. Wonderful showed up, and if he so much as looked at Zoe wrong, Dylan would be tossing him out the door. It was his job as her best friend to look after her. She was too innocent to spot a jerk, but he certainly had no trouble doing it. She might get mad at him, but he was just doing it for her own good, right?

Four

Dana ran into her office grinning from ear to ear. "Lisa just called and said that she was sure Dylan took the bait. She told him about your big date and what time Paul was supposed to arrive." Glancing down at her watch, she added, "That gives us half an hour to turn you into a woman who'll have them both swallowing their tongues. Now, did you bring the maxi dress?" Zoe pointed to the garment bag hanging behind her desk. She'd actually been surprised that Dana had picked a dress that came almost to her feet even with the heels she'd be wearing with it. She didn't remember much of anything else about it since she'd been so tired from shopping by that point that she'd agreed to anything Dana suggested. Dana unzipped the bag and pulled the silky fabric out before handing it to her. "Go ahead and put this on while I check on things out front. Then I'll be back to help you with your hair."

It was on the verge of Zoe's tongue to tell her that she'd managed on her own for years, then she remembered Dylan's reaction this morning. Obviously Dana knew way more about what men liked than she did. She reached over and locked the door before quickly stripping out of her work clothes. She pulled the long dress over her head and sighed in pleasure at how the slinky material felt against her skin. The neckline was a bit low, but not horrible. Turning to the side, she checked out her profile in the mirror she had on the wall, and that's when she noticed it. Oh God, how had she missed the fact in the store that it had a slit down one leg almost to her panty line. When Dana walked back in, Zoe wailed, "I can't wear this hoochie dress! If it rides up at all, my underwear will be showing. Why in the world did you let me buy it?" When she attempted to pull the dress down farther, it bared her breasts. There was no possible way to make any adjustments without exposing a body part.

Holding her hands up, Dana giggled, "Hey, you picked it out. I wondered about it, but you seemed determined." Dana studied her for a moment before saying, "It looks amazing, though. Paul is gonna choke when he gets a load of you in that. Plus, there's plenty of material in the skirt. When you sit down, just fold it over and you'll be covered. It won't gap open too much when you're walking, and you're not likely to run anywhere in those heels . . ."

Zoe crossed the floor several times and found that Dana was right. She could see flashes of her leg, but nothing X-rated. She had to admit that it was more than flattering and so very comfortable. She'd just be mindful of the split tonight and everything should be fine. "All right, I guess it's okay," she conceded before sitting again to pull on the strappy sandals she'd brought to match it. She still wasn't comfortable wobbling around in heels, but wow, they made her legs look endless, so maybe Dana was right about them being a necessary evil.

"Let's get to the makeup, then." Dana pulled something that resembled a suitcase from the corner and hefted it up onto the desk.

"What in the world is that?" Zoe asked.

"It's the holy grail, my dear," Dana replied as she unzipped the case and showed her tons of makeup as well as a flat iron, which she promptly plugged into a nearby outlet. "I thought we'd go the smooth route on the hair tonight and maybe a smoky eye for the makeup."

She had helped Zoe get ready for her dinner with Dylan the night before, but it had been with makeup that she had in her purse and a can of hairspray.

Obviously tonight she'd brought everything she owned with her. Zoe tried to back away, thinking she was in over her head, but the other woman caught her by the arm and backed her into a chair. "Oh, no you don't. I promise you'll love the end result. It'll look like you—only better."

Barely daring to breathe, Zoe sat perfectly still while Dana worked on first her face, then her hair. She was afraid if she moved she'd end up with third-degree burns from the huge flat iron Dana was wielding with such frightening speed. "Um . . . are you almost finished?" she dared to ask when Dana stepped back, studying her as she would a science experiment.

Giving Zoe a satisfied smirk, she said, "Oh, yeah, I've made a masterpiece. You should have both Dylan and Paul in some serious lust when they see you."

"You realize that I only care about Dylan's reaction, right?" Zoe pointed out. She had no intentions of seeing Paul again and thought of him as just a means to an end.

"Oh, sure," Dana agreed as she began packing her huge bag once again. "But you need some experience with men and the whole flirting thing. You've been one of the guys for too long. Now that you snagged Dylan's attention, you need to know how to handle it. You want him touching you like a woman, not popping his fist on your shoulder."

"That doesn't hurt," Zoe said defensively. "It's just our special thing that we do together."

Looking skeptical, Dana asked, "So, you've never seen him do that with any of his guy friends? It's only for you?"

Shifting in her chair, Zoe admitted, "Well, I guess it's more of a thing he does with his close friends. But he does it to me the most," she felt compelled to add.

Dana spoke slowly as if trying to get through to a child. "That's because you're with him the most, sweetie. That's not what you want from a man you're hot for. It's the universal guys' informal handshake or something like that. You want a man who goes in for a hug, like a full-body one. Or at the very least stares at your boobs until his eyes cross."

"He was doing that this morning," Zoe said, and grinned. "It wasn't for that long, but he was definitely looking at them. And sweating a lot again. I'm still afraid he's getting sick. I hope he does drop by so I can check on him."

Dana rolled her eyes. "He's fine. According to Lisa, he was playing Angry Birds with his feet propped on his desk. She said he's gotten lazy."

Before Zoe could reply, there was a knock on the door. Cat, their afternoon barista, stuck her head in to say, "There's a guy named Paul here to see you, Zoe." Wiggling her brows, she added, "Way to go. He's a total babe."

Zoe could feel herself blushing as she thanked Cat and took a deep breath to settle her nerves. She'd been so determined to make Dylan jealous that she hadn't really thought about the fact that she'd be forced to spend a whole evening with a virtual stranger. Even if Dana had suggested a movie, she still had to sit beside the man. What if he tried something? She hadn't had an actual date in ages. Dana was right—she desperately needed some experience in how to talk to a man because she had almost none. Turning to Dana, she whispered, "Maybe I should cancel. This is probably a big mistake."

Instead of answering her right away, Dana walked over to the door and cracked it open. She stood there for a moment before turning around to face her. "Guess what, babe? Dylan's here and sitting at the bar. He's only two stools away from Paul. Now, if you want to chicken out, I won't stop you, but you'd be missing a golden opportunity to make your man jealous. Just the fact that he's here tells me that he may not even know it yet, but he doesn't want you with anyone but him. You can either go out there and drive that point home or you can be content with whatever you guys have been doing for the past eighteen years. Totally up to you."

Biting her lip, Zoe knew her friend was right. And what was one evening out of her life? Paul was a friend of Dana's, so he wasn't likely to get out of hand. Plus, she worked with the public so she simply needed to call on her customer skills to survive the next few hours. She'd make polite conversation, enjoy a good meal and a movie. No problem. Squaring her shoulders, she marched toward Dana. "Let's do this," she muttered and saw the other woman beam her approval as they walked out to meet her date.

Zoe had to agree with Cat that Paul was more than a little good looking. But it was the man sitting a few seats away glaring at a seemingly oblivious Paul who had most of her attention. She wanted to stand and enjoy the notion that he was jealous, but Dana cleared her throat loudly before moving over to give her former boyfriend a hug. "Good to see you, honey. I see you're not slacking in the gym."

Paul crushed the petite woman to his chest for probably longer than was appropriate when your date was watching, but Zoe didn't really care. "Hey, baby. Have you ever known me to miss a day working out?"

Zoe heard Dylan mumble something under his breath, but couldn't catch what it was. Dana had finally put some distance between her and Paul and was proudly pointing to Zoe. "This is my friend that I told you about. Isn't she beautiful?"

Taking that question seriously, Paul looked at Zoe from head to foot, then back again before saying, "She's a knockout. Damn shame to waste all of that on another wo—"

Before he could complete his sentence, Dana planted her spiky heel on his foot, effectively stopping him from outing Zoe as a lesbian. Paul was hopping up and down, howling in pain while Dana pretended to be sorry that she was so clumsy. The whole thing looked like a circus. Dylan was shaking his head in confusion, while Zoe pretended not to notice the glances he was shooting her way. "I'm so sorry, sugar, I'm a big old klutz. Thank goodness you're such a tough guy and can handle a little bit of pain." Dana's backhanded compliment seemed to be just what Paul needed to recoup.

He gave Dana a side hug, again holding it for a bit too long. "It's nothing, honey. You're so light I barely felt it."

Zoe had to fight the urge to gag since he'd been staggering around just moments ago as if he were dying. She reluctantly crossed to his side when Dylan got to his feet. His eyes widened and he appeared to be staring at her feet. Looking down, she immediately knew what had his attention. Her purse strap had somehow gotten entangled in her skirt, pulling the long slit apart and exposing an obscene amount of flesh. She was pretty sure the edge of her panties was even visible. Luckily Paul had been too caught up in Dana to notice yet. She quickly untangled the strap and tugged the fabric closed. "Maybe you should go change," Dylan hissed, not appearing satisfied that she was once again covered.

"It's fine." She waved him off with more confidence than she felt.

"Don't you have one of your old uniforms in your office?" he suggested.

Dana, having obviously overheard him, piped up loudly, "No, she doesn't." She grabbed Zoe's arm and pulled her away from Dylan. "You two should get going. Don't do anything I wouldn't do," she added, which of course, probably confused the hell out of Paul since he thought Zoe batted for the other team.

Dylan trailed them, but he didn't stand a chance against a determined Dana. She literally propelled them out the door. Despite herself, Zoe was impressed. Her petite friend could take on anyone. Or at least she hoped so, because Dylan was scowling so fiercely, Zoe was afraid Dana would need some soothing words to placate him. She couldn't worry about that now. She had hours to survive with a man who thought she was gay, who was still hung up on Dana, and whom she had nothing at all in common with. Let the fun begin.

$\sim$

Dylan stared incredulously after his best friend and the asshole who was her date for the night. He couldn't believe that Zoe had left with him, considering the man had groped Dana right in front of her. When the douche bag had walked in the shop, he'd sauntered up to the bar like he owned the place before looking at Dylan and saying, "S'up, bro." He'd hoped like hell at that moment that this wasn't the guy she was supposed to be going out with.

Apparently the jock had more muscles than intelligence. Dylan had seen the type around the gym and beach. The ones who worked out three hours a day, then sat around waiting for ladies to drop their panties for them. His Zoe wasn't that type of woman. But what in the hell was she wearing? He was positive he saw her panties from the big split in that dress. He swallowed hard. She looked incredible. Which stirred up all kinds of conflicting emotions for him. He was stunned that he'd never noticed exactly how gorgeous she was before. And strangely proud of how she'd blossomed into a beautiful butterfly. He also felt fiercely protective. What if this idiot tried to take advantage of her? There was no way she was strong enough to fight him off. He was probably hyped up on steroids and whatever else he could find. Shit, he could go into some kind of rage over the smallest of things.

Dylan put his hands on his hips and glared at Dana. He knew he needed to keep his voice down because there were customers not far away, but right now he had a hard time caring. "Why in God's name would you fix Zoe up with him? Have you lost your mind?"

Despite being a foot taller than her, Dylan could tell he wasn't intimidating her in the least. She laughed—

actually laughed—in his face then cuffed him on the shoulder. Had the whole world gone insane tonight? "Paul's a sweetheart, Dylan. Zoe will have a great time with him." Fanning herself, she added, "Didn't she look hot tonight? Paul is going to be thanking me later for sure."

"Wh-what? Er . . . yes, she looked very nice. But that's really not the point here. What do you know about this Paul? Because I don't trust him. Do you know where they were going? I should probably swing by and make sure everything's okay."

"Nope, don't have a clue," Dana said airily. "In case you've missed it, though, Zoe's a grown woman and more than capable of taking care of herself. And I dated Paul for several months so I can vouch for him. I mean, he's into some kinky stuff once he gets things fired up, but hey, most women like that now. I bet you've had some dates that were freaks, huh?" *Why does she keep punching my shoulder like we're buddies?*

Irritated at her nonchalant attitude, he snapped, "We're not talking about me here. Can you please focus for a minute?" When she continued to grin at him stupidly, he pulled his phone from his jacket pocket and hit the speed dial for Zoe. The damn thing rang once and went right to voice mail. "Fuck." He waited for the tone and left a message. "Hey, it's me. Can you give me a call back as soon as you get this?" Ending the call, he looked over to see an amused Dana watching him. "That's what you should have been doing," he growled. "If you hear from her, tell her I'm trying to reach her. Can you at least do that?"

She actually rolled her eyes before waving off his concerns as if they were nothing. "Oh, relax, Papa Bear, everything's cool. There is absolutely nothing to get your briefs in a wad over, I can assure you. She'll have a great evening, and if she plays her cards right, it'll extend into the next morning."

He felt physically sick at her words. If she thought that was supposed to be reassuring, she was dead wrong. "If that happens, I'm holding your personally responsible," he warned before stalking out the door.

What in the fuck was happening around here? He'd been home for a day and everything had changed. He barely recognized Zoe anymore and she was on some kind of dating marathon to boot. He kept feeling like he was the only one missing out on a joke that no one would explain to him, and he hated it. Since when was he out of the loop with his best friend? And Dana . . . He wanted to wrap his hands around her neck and strangle her. Being laughed at and heckled in his own hotel wasn't something he was used to. In yet another first, he figured he might as well go for broke and head home to stare at his phone while he waited for Zoe to call him back. He'd always laughed at his pussy-whipped buddies who did shit like that, and now he was joining their leagues and there was no sex involved. This was all Zoe's fault, he fumed as he stalked out. She was too young to be having a midlife crisis so he wasn't sure what to call her little walk on the wild side. All he knew was it was going to stop if he had anything to say about it. Tomorrow he'd lay down the law. She had always been a sensible woman, and he was sure when he explained how crazy her recent behavior had been, she'd see that he was right and revert to her old self. Because if she didn't, he wasn't sure he'd survive another week.

Five

Dana had already been at the shop when Zoe arrived. The other woman had literally been bouncing on her heels with excitement. "I swear, Zoe, you should have seen Dylan after you guys left last night. He was like a caged tiger being taunted with a feather duster. It was hilarious. I actually thought he was going to do me bodily harm a few times. If there hadn't been so many witnesses around, I'm not so sure he wouldn't have."

Yawning, Zoe gratefully accepted the vanilla latte from Dana and took a sip. "Sorry I didn't call you last night, but we went to a movie that was over three hours long and it didn't start until nine. It was well after midnight by the time I got home. Why would

Paul pick some war movie, then sleep through most of it?"

Smiling fondly, Dana said, "He always did fall asleep while we were watching television. He works out from three to five in the mornings so he was tired by the afternoon. If we were going to be out late, I made him take a nap first."

"I don't suppose your big evening out included dinner at Subway, did it? I must say I was a bit surprised by that. Don't get me wrong, I love a good sub sandwich, but it wasn't quite what I was expecting. I even made it known when we got in the car that I'd be paying my own way."

Dana wrinkled her nose. "Yeah, I've tried to tell him that you can get way better meals at nicer restaurants, but he's convinced that's not true. Plus, apparently he's addicted to that damn Black Forest ham. Do they put crack in that or something?"

Laughing, Zoe set her cup down before her latte spilled over the sides. "You should have seen his face when I ordered the large popcorn with extra butter and a Coke. He got a bottle of water and some low-carb snack pack they had that consisted of a few cashews and some cheese. He even had the nerve to suggest that my 'girlfriend' might have broken up with me over my eating habits. I told him that she ate even more than me, and I swear, he looked kind of nauseous."

Smirking, Dana asked, "So I'm guessing you didn't

have any issues with him hitting on you?" Zoe was surprised to see that her friend looked more than a little anxious as she waited for her to answer. Could she still have feelings for her ex? They'd certainly been very friendly last night in the shop. And Paul had talked about her on and off all evening. She thought he was still smitten with Dana and it looked as if the feeling might be mutual.

Deciding to test her theory, she lowered her voice and motioned Dana closer. When she was just inches away, Zoe said, "He couldn't keep his hands off me during the movie. Do you think it was because I was supposed to be gay? Maybe he figured it was a challenge—you know, bring me back to the other side." Twirling a piece of her hair, she added, "He's pretty hot too. What a body. I mean, I know you said he had a small . . . you know, but does that really matter? He's got other . . . um, tools to work with, and if he would stop taking the steroids, he'd be more eager to experiment, right?" A quick glance showed Dana's face had turned to stone. Zoe didn't think she'd even taken a breath since she'd started teasing her. "He did mention wanting to see me again, so I might find out for myself soon!"

Apparently that last line was the final straw because Dana jerked upright, sputtering, "What—no. That wasn't the agreement. He was on loan to you. It wasn't a real date; don't you remember? You're in love with Dylan. Paul isn't even your type." When Zoe didn't react, Dana shrilled, "Do you want to eat at Subway for the rest of your life?"

"Calm down," Zoe giggled. "I have no desire to take your man. Because that's exactly what he is. I have no idea why you really broke up with him, but it's clear you've still got feelings for him, and considering he said your name about a hundred times last night, I'd say it's mutual. So what gives there? Are you really that hung up on his, um . . . package? I certainly would hope that Dylan has a good-size thing down there, but if we ever got together and I discovered that he didn't, I wouldn't dump him over it. It's not like that's something a man has any control over."

"He said he never wanted any kids," Dana blurted out. "Actually he called them brats, which is even worse."

"Hate to point it out, Dana, but you call them the same thing. Isn't that a little pot and kettle?"

"I know," Dana huffed, "but I still want them someday. We had a talk about the future one night, and even though he said he hoped we'll still be together, that was it. No marriage, no kids, or any kind of change for that matter. I think he's perfectly content to run his gym and date. Which is fine right now, but we're not exactly kids. Shouldn't he have some goals?"

"Well, he has his own business," Zoe pointed out. "So it's not as if he's a slacker. That had to have taken careful planning to start and to maintain. Trust me, something like that is your baby for a long time. It's possible he wasn't putting as much thought into the future as you were at that time. He may have been feeling overwhelmed by the business and said the first thing that came to mind. Plus, let's face it, sometimes men aren't as sensitive and in tune with our feelings as we'd like them to be." Grimacing, she added, "I wouldn't be going through this whole circus with Dylan if he'd picked up on any of my thoughts, that's for sure. So you should talk to Paul. Get everything out in the open. Oh, wait—you're dating someone else. Should you break up with him before or after you talk to Paul? It would be kinda wrong to wait, like keeping your options open in case Paul doesn't say what you want to hear."

Shrugging her shoulders, Dana said, "Mike and I broke up last night, so that's not a problem."

"Oh my God," Zoe cried, "why didn't you tell me? Are you all right? Here I was going on and on and you've had a breakup." Looking around behind the counter frantically, she added, "I think I've got a chocolate bar here somewhere. Will that help?"

"Sweetie, it's really not a big deal," Dana said calmly. "It wasn't going anywhere and I never wanted it to. He was a rebound thing to get over Paul—which obviously hasn't worked so well. Last night I was telling him about you going out with him and apparently my jealousy came through loud and clear. Mike's a very sweet guy and he said he never understood why I'd broken up with Paul in the first place and maybe I needed some time to get my thoughts together. That was it. No big scene or angry words. We're still friends and will stay that way."

Zoe was more impressed than she could say. It all sounded so very adult to her. "Wow, it's amazing how that worked out. So you're free and so is Paul. What are you going to do about it?"

A regular mothers' group came in before the other woman could answer, and by the time they'd served them and other customers who trickled in behind them, almost an hour had passed. Dana walked by on the way to the kitchen and paused. "That last question you asked?" Holding up her arm, she flexed her muscles. "I think I'm going for a little workout tomorrow morning. You can burn a lot of calories doing naughty things on the reception desk, you know. But in the meantime, how about a girls' night? You order the pizza and I'll bring the wine—a bottle for each of us."

Giving her friend a high five, Zoe said, "You got yourself a deal. Plus, it'll give me something to do since Dylan's volunteering for Habitat for Humanity today. And he usually meets his friends for dinner on Thursdays."

Dana shook her head. "I swear, you should be married to that man. You know his schedule better than he does. Anyway, I'll be over about seven tonight. We can plan your next move, although I don't know how much more we'll need. If last night was any indication, Dylan's going to fold like a house of cards soon. I give him another week max."

Zoe could only hope her friend was right because otherwise the only move left was telling him how she felt and it would take more than Dana's bottle of wine for her to do that. Their next plan had to be brilliant. She felt a twinge of guilt at the deception, but quickly brushed it aside. All was fair in love and war and this might be a little of both before it was over with.

Dylan was tired and irritable when he arrived at Zoe's condo around ten that evening. He'd spent the day with several other Oceanix employees working on a Habitat for Humanity house on the other side of town. He volunteered as often as he could, and even though he'd been distracted with Zoe for the last few days, he always honored his commitments. Normally, he met some friends for a beer on Thursday, but everyone it seemed had scheduling conflicts tonight, which was fine by him. He'd been playing phone tag with Zoe all day and he didn't plan to let another night pass without getting to the bottom of her strange behavior. Hell, he'd barely slept, thanks to her. He was tired, irritable, and distracted. At this point, he knew all he'd accomplish at the office tomorrow would be more hours expended on Angry Birds because that's about the only thing he did other than obsess over his best friend. That had to stop. It was messing with his whole life.

When he stepped out of the elevator, he heard music blaring. For a moment, he thought it was her neighbor, who traveled a lot but liked to entertain when she was home. As he walked closer to Zoe's door, though, he realized it was actually coming from her place. Why would she be having a party on a work night? That was absurd. *Shit, I'm really starting to sound old.* Shrugging that thought aside, he pressed the doorbell. When no one answered, he did it twice more before giving up. He doubted she could hear him over all the noise. He pulled his keys from his pocket and quickly located the spare that he kept for her. When either of them was out of town, the other always checked on things while they were gone.

He tried the bell one last time before fitting the key in the lock and opening the door. What he saw had him blinking in shock. Maybe he was more sleep deprived than he realized. Because unless he was hallucinating, Zoe was pole dancing while Dana shook her hips and shouted directions. Holy mother, his best friend was wearing skimpy shorts and a tank top while she ground her hips against a shiny bar. Dylan swallowed hard, but it did nothing to ease the lump in his throat or the rapidly growing bulge in his pants. Looking to the heavens for a brief moment, he mouthed, *What else, God?* before turning back to process what he was seeing. "Um . . . hello," he announced, attempting to be heard over the noise. Neither woman acted as if they'd heard him. By this point, Zoe appeared to be kissing the pole. *What the hell?*

"That's right, work it, girl," Dana yelled in encouragement. "Get in there and show him who's boss. Shake that moneymaker."

Moneymaker? This was getting out of hand fast. He was both afraid and hopeful that Zoe would start stripping next. Fuck, if that happened, he wasn't sure what would become of him. He was so hard now, his cock was digging into his zipper through his boxers. "Hello!" he bellowed out and was thankful to see both women jerk and look his way.

"Hey, Dylan." Dana staggered over and attempted to hug him. He held an arm out, keeping some space between them as he attempted to pry her hands off his chest. Suddenly she pulled back and wrinkled her nose. "You smell sweaty," she stated as if she didn't reek of booze. "Hey, Zoe, look who's here," she sing-songed. "It's your Pooh Bear."

This was getting worse by the moment. Zoe was weaving on her feet as she gave him what he guessed was a drunken grin. "Hey, Dylan," she shouted. "We're dancing! Dana has a porta-pole thingie." *Of course she does,* he thought wryly as he waved in return before walking over to the iPod docking station and turning the music off. It was eerily quiet now and he almost wished he'd left it on low. Then there was the sound of someone burping followed by a giggle. *Dear God, give me strength.*

"All right, ladies, party's over. I'll take Dana home, then I'll come back and make sure you're okay, Zoe. You're too drunk to be alone." He knew the trip would probably be hell with someone so obviously wasted, but he really just wanted Dana gone.

He was halfway to the kitchen when Dana called out, "Paul's on his way to pick me up so I don't need a ride. Well, at least not the kind you're offering." Another round of giggling accompanied that lewd statement and he stood with his back to them for a moment, until he'd worked up the courage to turn around.

"Paul as in your date from last night?" he asked Zoe. He couldn't say that he was surprised. The man had plainly been a dirtball.

"He was mine first," Dana tossed out, "and we're back together. But it's okay, 'cause I'm getting Zoe an even better one."

How attached is Zoe to her employee? Because I'm ready to buy her a one-way ticket to anywhere but here. Struggling to remain calm, Dylan bit out quietly, "I think you've helped out quite enough. You and your boyfriend or whatever the hell he is need to leave Zoe alone."

Dana put her hands on her hips, slurring out, "You'd like that, wouldn't you. Then you could have her all to yourself." Then she got right in his face, wagging her finger so hard he wouldn't have been surprised to see it pop off. "She's got a life other than you now, big boy. If you want to spend time with her, then you got to schedule ahead. She's not your back-end . . . backdoor . . ." While he was trying to figure out what she was trying to say, she let out a series of hiccups before yelling, "Backup plan!"

As if sensing his rising temper, the other woman wobbled away. Following behind her more slowly, he asked, "Do you need to call your *boyfriend* and let him know you're ready to go?" *Please let her be leaving before I'm forced to hide her body tonight.*

He sighed in relief when she said, "I already texted him."

Out of the corner of his eye, he saw Zoe begin to sway on her feet. She still had the same stoned grin on her face, but she looked a little paler than she had a few moments ago. He crossed to her and was a few inches away when she launched herself at him. For someone drunk, she was surprisingly strong and agile as she wrapped her arms around his neck and her legs around his waist. He automatically put his arms around her to keep her from falling. *This is so not good,* he thought as his now semi-erect dick took notice of the new situation immediately. "Hey, best friend," she cooed as she snuggled closer. "You feel good—so hard."

Her cheek was against his chest so he could only hope she was talking about those muscles and not his dick with that last word. "Um . . . Zoe, let me put you on the sofa. It'll be more comfortable." But as he bent over and removed his hands, she stubbornly held on. *Shit, when did she get so strong?* She hung on to him like a monkey, and nothing short of prying her off was going to work. So instead, he straightened, having no idea what to do next.

Dylan was almost certain she sniffed him, which if what Dana said about the sweat smell earlier was true, then it might not have been a great idea. "Mmm, I think I'll just stay right—"

When she stopped mid-sentence, he looked down just as a soft snore sounded from her mouth. *Don't think about how adorable she looks in your arms, she's your best friend—that's all.*

He was jerked from his musings as someone banged on the door. No doubt it was Paul, who couldn't be bothered to use the buzzer. "That's my baby." Dana ran through the apartment. Dylan was pretty sure she'd nodded off to sleep as well since she hadn't been in his face in at least two minutes. He thought of warning her to check the peephole first, then decided that he didn't really care as long as whoever was on the other side took her with them. But a few seconds later, he could tell it was Paul by the amount of groping and tonsil sucking going on in the hallway.

"Good night—shut the door," He called to them and was pleasantly surprised when it actually worked.

Dylan didn't care if she'd left her purse and whatever the hell she brought with her, she wasn't getting back in tonight. She'd probably screw her jock boyfriend right there in the elevator for all to see. Again, not his problem.

The warm body pressed against his begin to wiggle around. He rocked her soothingly, thinking maybe she was having a bad dream or something even though she'd barely been asleep long enough for that to happen. "Rock a bye baaabbby," she began to sing. It was so bad, he thought his ears might bleed, but he found himself chuckling anyway.

She didn't appear to be inclined to let go of him anytime soon, so he turned around and plopped down on the sofa. He thought that had probably been a mistake when that put them almost face-to-face. How had he never noticed how gorgeous her big brown eyes were before? And those lips. Soft, pink, and so perfectly plump. It was taking everything he had not to lean down and see if they tasted as good as they looked. He knew he was screwed when her teeth clamped down on the lower lip as she stared at him. Dammit, he was sweating again. He'd probably lost five pounds of fluid in the last few days from that nervous habit alone. She reached out to touch his forehead about the time he gently began tracing her lip and trying to remove her teeth from the tender flesh. "Let go honey before you hurt yourself," he instructed raggedly.

"You're flushed again," she whispered as she stroked his face. "Are you sure you haven't picked up a bug of some kind? I don't think it's anything sexually transmitted because I don't believe you'd sweat—at least not up there."

When she looked down toward his crotch, he had to resist the urge to clamp a hand over it. Clearing his throat, he said, "I can assure you that everything's in top condition and there's no problems under the hood, so to speak."

She nodded, then gave him a toothy grin. "That's good to hear." She let her head fall against him once again before saying, "At least you have that possibility. You know, that you could have HD or something."

"HD?" he asked in confusion. Then it hit him. "Er . . . I think you mean VD, as in 'venereal disease,' and I don't think there's any possibility of that, sweetheart. I'm a safety-first kinda guy. I always wrap it up. Never gone bareback before. Don't want any little Dylans out there running around that I don't know about." *Why am I rattling on about this? Fuck, just shut up already. You're making yourself sound like a man whore.*

"That's good." She patted his chest. "I'll have to remember that if I ever get that far with a man. I mean, don't get me wrong, I've made out before," she slurred, "but that's it. Guess you could say I've been to second base. Wait, what is second base exactly?" Before Dylan could answer, she plowed on. "If third base is touching the downstairs area—you know under the clothes, then

I haven't been to that one yet. And no one has slid into my home base." Looking up at him suddenly, she added, "That's code for sex, in case you didn't know. Going all the way and everything." She collapsed limply back against him, and he heard another soft snore.

There was no way he could let her revelation pass without clarification. He used a hand to shake her gently. "Zoe, are you trying to say you're a virgin?" They'd been friends their entire adult life so of course he knew she didn't date much. But there had been both of their college years when they'd lost touch at times. She'd mention some guy she was seeing and he had always assumed there was sex involved. He hadn't particularly liked it even back then because he'd always felt protective where she was concerned. She was his best friend, after all, and he didn't want some bastard taking advantage of her. He knew she'd been extremely busy in recent years making a success of her business and didn't have time for a man in her life. He'd had no problem with that since it meant she was usually free to hang out when he wanted to. *I'm such a selfish bastard.*

"Huh?" she mumbled when he jarred her again. "Oh, yep, I'm a virgin. Probably the oldest one still left in Florida." She was drifting off again, but her last words were enough to turn him to ice. "But I'm going to do something about that before I'm thirty. Giving it to someone special."

No way in hell. His mind had officially been blown.

Zoe was still a virgin and she'd decided to change that status by her next birthday? The sudden change in her appearance and the increase in her social life made a horrifying kind of sense now. And Dylan couldn't let it happen. What she obviously viewed as a bad thing, he thought was amazing. She was almost thirty and had never been with a man. Why in the world would she want to give something so precious away to a stranger? Fuck, what if she'd slept with that loser Paul?

He absently pressed a kiss to the top of her head while he pondered the dilemma. He'd had his cherry popped years ago, so he'd never put much thought into it after that. For most guys it was fairly simple. From the moment you were old enough to figure out the difference between the sexes, you used most of your brain cells hoping a chick would say yes. If you're lucky as you gain maturity, you're a little smoother, but the end goal is the same—sex. Dylan wasn't a vain man, but he had to admit that wooing a woman had never been a problem for him. There was usually one available whenever he wanted. Hell, it would take him an embarrassingly long time to sit down and count his past partners. He wasn't even sure he could. It was hard for him to fathom how the woman he held in his arms could be so innocent.

Sure, she didn't exactly go out of her way to attract men. She'd never been a flashy dresser. He wouldn't call it bad; it was simply Zoe. She wasn't out to impress anyone. Her usual wardrobe was filled with coffee-stained white polo shirts. She barely wore makeup—actually he wasn't sure she wore any. And he didn't need to look beneath her clothes to know she was a plain cotton panties type of gal. In truth, it was one of the reasons their friendship worked. He could relax with her. Hell, he could fart in front of her and not spend an hour apologizing. She'd laugh, throw a pillow at him, and that was the end of it. He'd scratch his ass when he wanted and so would she. It was comfort all the way when they were together. *But what if I could have all that and the girl?* No sooner had the thought occurred than Dylan was striking it down. That was impossible. Something like that would make Zoe the perfect woman, which would mean he'd overlooked her for years. Impossible. He wasn't that stupid or blind . . . was he?

He carefully moved a hand from around her and rubbed his throbbing temple. She was doing a real number on him. He was tired and confused. That was the reason he was thinking irrationally. He simply needed to have a talk with her—preferably when she was sober—and give her his opinion on this whole getting-rid-of-her-virginity business. She'd always been a rational woman, and he was sure he could get her to see reason.

Dylan blamed this whole mess on that trouble-maker Dana. How dare she fill Zoe's head with nonsense? He was certain she was behind this rush to find a man. For fuck's sake, she'd even set her up with her boyfriend. He knew that Dana was a friend as well as an employee, but she damn sure wasn't a good influence. The whole drunken dirty dancing tonight was just further proof of that. Dylan studied the pole that Zoe had been grinding on a short time ago. Where had that thing come from? It certainly hadn't been here last week. Dana probably carried it around in her car for impromptu striptease opportunities.

Dropping his head onto the back of the sofa, he stifled a yawn. *So very tired.* As soon as Zoe woke up, they'd straighten this mess out. But for now, he was going to rest his eyes until he had the desire and the energy to move her from his lap and go home.

Six

Why does my bed sound like a train? Zoe wondered fuzzily as she shifted, attempting to get comfortable. Her body was stiff and she was burning up. Plus, what was rumbling beneath her ear? Reaching her hands out, she felt around experimentally. Hmmm, this was interesting. She appeared to be lying on something. *What?*

She was a flurry of scurrying elbows and knees as she attempted to open her eyes against the bright glare in the room. "Shit, stop before you kill me," hissed a voice that she immediately recognized. *No, that can't be right. Why would he be here? Wait . . . Is there a hand on my ass?*

That did it. Zoe's eyes popped open and she was

staring directly into Dylan's face. Where did he come from? His sleepy eyes and facial scruff indicated that he'd probably been there for a while. And more importantly, why was he underneath her? *Maybe I'm still asleep and this is a dream. That must be it.* Well, heck, if that was the case, she was going to enjoy it. She'd had a lot of sex dreams about her best friend through the years, but this one was so vivid. Of course, even her dreams weren't perfect. She actually had a headache and a bit of a dry mouth. But who cared? Dylan was in her bed. No, actually they were on the sofa. Gazing down at his beautiful face, she could hardly decide what she wanted to do first. She only knew she better hurry before she woke up alone as usual. *Pucker up, BFF, I'm coming in for a kiss.* "Oh, Dylan," she whispered before she lowered her lips to his.

His body jerked against hers, but whatever he said was quickly muffled as her tongue entered his mouth. *This is so hot*, she thought as she allowed her hands and tongue to roam free. Surely the real thing couldn't be much better than this. And she didn't have to worry about feeling shy or awkward because this wasn't really happening. The hand on her ass was squeezing now, and strangely enough, she felt his nails digging into the tender flesh there. The twinge of pain amplified the heady desire rushing through her body and she was almost certain that a dry-humping dream orgasm was right round the corner.

That is, until she went sailing through the air and ended up several feet away from the object of her lust. *What the hell?* Usually she just woke up. Now she had men tossing her on the floor in her dreams? Geez, what was next, restraining orders? Suddenly, Dylan was down on his haunches peering at her in concern. "Shit, Zoe, are you all right? I didn't know it was real. I thought it was a dream."

Rubbing her elbow where it had struck the hardwood floor, she flinched. "Seems like more of a nightmare now."

"You were kissing me," he said accusingly. "And your hands were . . . on everything. I was startled and it was a knee-jerk reaction."

"Oh, calm down," she chided. "It'll all be over in a minute. This happens to me all the time. Although nothing quite this realistic."

Looking exasperated, he asked, "Are you still drunk? It's been hours. How much did you two put away last night?"

He was making absolutely no sense. As she tried to decipher his strange words, she glanced around and then did a double take. "Er . . . why is there a pole in my living room?" Then, as if watching a movie in slow motion, it all came back to her. Dana bringing over two bottles of wine and her portable stripper pole. Apparently she'd ordered it and the instructional DVD off one of those late-night shows. They'd cranked up the music and Zoe had let her inner stripper loose. That answered the question of why her thighs were so damn sore. But where did Dylan fit into all of this? "Why are you here?" she finally asked, giving up on figuring it out on her own.

Interestingly enough, he looked uncomfortable now. Well, even more so than the already strange occurrences called for. "I dropped by on my way home last night. When I got here, I could hear the music blaring all the way down the hall. I tried the doorbell several times, but no one answered. So I used my key to make sure everything was okay. Um . . . that's when I found you two in here dancing and three sheets to the wind. You were on that thing," he said, pointing to the pole. She thought she must be seeing things, because he actually appeared to be blushing. *Please, God, tell me I had clothes on during that dance.*

"O-kay," she said carefully. "So how did I go from that to sleeping on top of you on the sofa?" *Oh my God, I totally kissed and groped Dylan!* She felt her own face flush as she realized what she'd done just moments earlier. No wonder he was having a hard time making eye contract. She'd probably totally freaked him out.

He took a moment to sit down, putting his back against the sofa in question. "I picked you up because you were wobbling all over the place. Then you fell asleep and I sat down with you in my arms. The next thing I knew, we were both awake and your . . . tongue was in my mouth. It er . . . startled me for a moment, which brings us to now."

Zoe dropped her head into her hands as she mumbled, "You tossed me off you like a rag doll because I was attacking you. If this isn't rock bottom, I don't know what is."

She felt him patting her shoulder, like any good friend would, which only made it that much more humiliating. "Zoe, it's really no big deal. You're used to waking up alone, so of course you were confused. And I was startled because you're not usually doing . . . all those things to me. It was a moment of temporary insanity on both our parts because I'd certainly never toss you off the sofa under normal circumstances."

Zoe did her best to put on a brave front, not wanting him to see how crushed she was by his reaction to her touch. "Let's just forget it." She raised her head and gave him a forced smile. Glancing at the nearby clock, she saw it was after seven. Thank God it wasn't her day to open early and luckily it wasn't Dana's either. "I'm sure you need to head home so you can get ready for work, and I could use a long shower too." *Maybe I'll drown myself in there. It would probably be less painful than this.*

As she began to get to her feet, she was startled when his hand shot out and stopped her. "I—I wanted to talk to you. How about I go pick us up a coffee and some of those sugar donuts you like while you take a shower. I have a while before my first appointment this morning, so if you can spare the time, there's something I really need to speak to you about."

He had her curiosity up now, which made it almost impossible to say no. She figured he'd be running out of here at top speed to escape the train wreck that was her coming on to him. But apparently the man was a glutton for punishment this morning. Plus, he did offer to get her food. How bad could it be? She'd already maxed out the embarrassment factor this morning so it was surely all uphill from this point on. "Sure," she nodded. "I'm out of sugar, though, so make sure you get extra put in my coffee and plenty of cream."

Dylan laughed as he got to his feet and extended a hand to help her up. "I know what you like, Zoe."

You sure do, Zoe couldn't help thinking. Especially if that kiss was any indication. She might have all but mauled him, but he'd certainly had some tongue of his own in her mouth before he threw her across the room. Dammit, her nipples were hardening just thinking about it. She quickly crossed her arms over the saluting girls and began backing up toward the bathroom. "I'm just going to . . . yeah, take that shower now. You have your key, so let yourself back in. Don't worry, I won't come out naked or anything. I'm afraid you might call the cops or something this time." *Crap, crap, crap. Why did I say that?*

Dylan stared at her for a moment, before giving her

an uncertain smile. "I'll be back soon. Take your time." And thankfully he was gone. He'd slept in all his clothes along with his shoes last night. While she was wearing her skimpiest shorts and a tank top that was two sizes too small. It did make her tits look big, though, which was why she'd kept it all these years. *And why does that matter when no one other than Dana has ever seen you in it?*

Zoe had no intention of still being in the shower when Dylan got back so she made quick work of bathing. She pulled on a pair of her new blue jean shorts, along with a slinky, open-shouldered top in purple. She threw her damp hair into a ponytail and added the hoop earrings she'd grown fond of wearing. She heard Dylan calling her name, so she skipped the makeup for now in favor of a light coat of moisturizer. When she walked into the kitchen, her stomach rumbled loudly at the smell of coffee and donuts. He'd already settled onto a stool at the bar and was sipping his own morning brew. She took a drink from her foam cup and moaned in bliss when the creamy, sweet liquid hit her tongue. "Mmm, this tastes amazing. Please never tell anyone that I'm addicted to Dunkin' Donuts. I'd never live it down."

He handed her one of the sugar-covered pastries and smiled indulgently when she took a huge bite. "You've got some on your chin," he pointed out as he reached out to wipe it away. When he put his finger in his mouth and sucked the sweetness off, Zoe felt her clit jump to attention. He'd done that a million times before, so why was it such a turn-on today? Ah hell, the man could probably pick his nose and belch the National Anthem and she'd still be sitting here drooling over him like a lovesick fool.

"So, what did you want to talk about?" she asked around her mouthful of deliciousness. She needed to do something to derail her hormonally overloaded brain before she orgasmed on the spot. *He's sweating again! Oh, dear God, he's going to tell me he's sick. That would explain so much.* The remains of her breakfast fell from her nerveless fingers as her stomach churned. "Dylan, what's going on? You're seriously beginning to freak me out."

"I know your big secret, Zoe, and why you've made all these changes. This sudden urge to date every night makes perfect, but twisted, sense to me now."

She could feel the color drain from her face. *I swear I'll kill Dana. I don't care if she was drunk or not, how could she tell him how I feel?* Zoe was doing her best to come up with some explanation for damage control, but so far had nothing. *Maybe I should go ahead and get it out there. No sense denying it now.*

She had opened her mouth to tell him everything, when he blurted out, "You told me last night that you're still a virgin." *So not where I thought he was going with this*. Silence. Nothing but complete and utter silence for so long as Zoe stared, dumbfounded.

"I—okay," she finally replied. "Not sure what you want me to say here." *Floor, open up and swallow me whole. Phone, ring. Pipes, burst. Please, anything to create a diversion so I can escape the most awkward moment of my life.* But as usual, the universe ignored her pleas for help and left her exactly where she was—facing her best friend, who now knew she qualified for nun status. Well, except for her potty mouth. *At least he doesn't know you're in love with him. That's something.*

Dylan rubbed his forehead as he always did when he was rattled. "Shit," he finally sighed. "I'm just going to lay it out there. I don't want you sleeping with some dirt bag just to get your cherry popped. Er . . . I mean, to get experience. You've waited for twenty-nine years and your first time should be with someone who cares about you."

Relying on humor to lessen the tension, Zoe smirked before rolling her eyes. "It's not as if I planned to do it in the back of a Buick, Dylan. I'd at least expect the man to spring for a room at Howard Johnson's."

Dylan's lips twitched before he became somber once again. "I mean it, Zoe. I realize that this is personal and probably not any of my business, but you know I love you. Even if I don't tell you that often enough."

She melted at his words, wishing he meant them in some way other than friendship or, God forbid, the sisterly type of affection. "I love you too, Dylan," she replied. "And I really appreciate you looking out for me. No matter what, I can always depend on you."

He nodded, looking pleased with her response. He appeared to take a deep breath, which had her bracing. It did absolutely no good, though, because she was rocked to her core with his next statement. "Good, because I think I should be your first. We both love and respect each other, so it's the perfect solution, don't you think?"

Zoe felt as if the floor had been pulled out from under her. Was he actually saying he wanted them to have sex? Her gut reaction was to jump up and down while pumping her fist and yelling, "Yes, yes, yes!" But somehow that seemed a little too enthusiastic for the controlled way that he was presenting the idea. Maybe she should tell him she'd ponder it and e-mail him later. Okay, that might be too nonchalant. But how in the heck were you supposed to react when your secret love/best friend offered to deflower you? Was there a *Losing Your Virginity for Dummies* that she could buy? Needing to clarify that she'd understood him correctly, she asked, "So you're saying you want to . . . do the deed with me?" *Way to go. You sound like a teenage boy.*

He grinned, looking so heart-stoppingly handsome that Zoe had to swallow the sudden lump in her throat. He really was a gorgeous man and so flipping sexy. She wanted to crawl across the table and lick his dimples. "Well, I'd prefer to think of it as making love with you. But yeah, that's the general idea." *He said "making love." Surely, that means something.* "We love each other, so I believe that would translate into the special night that you deserve for your first time."

Suddenly this wasn't sounding as good. If she understood him correctly, this was a one-shot deal. There was no indication that he had any type of feelings for her other than friendship, nor did he plan to change their relationship from what it currently was. He wanted to be her first simply to keep her from sleeping with a stranger. He had no idea that she was only pretending to date to snag his interest. Well, she appeared to have that, but not exactly in the way she'd intended. *Now what?* She finally settled on, "Wow, I don't know what to say."

"Why don't you take some time to think it over," he suggested. "But I'd really prefer that you didn't sleep with anyone else until we talk again."

Shaking her head, she said wryly, "I've waited this long, Dylan, it's not likely I'm going to drop my panties for just anyone. I do have a few standards, you know. I think I'm capable of keeping myself under control for a few days."

He tossed a donut crumb off the table at her. "Smart-ass."

She couldn't stop herself from asking something she was very curious about. "So how would this work exactly? You'd come over and we'd have sex, then we'd go on as if nothing had happened?"

He appeared thoughtful as if really considering her words. Apparently, he hadn't thought the details out before making the proposal. Finally, he said, "I believe it would be a good idea to lead up to it a bit, so you'll be more comfortable. We already spend a lot of time together, but this would be a little different. We could go out for dinner. Come back and have a glass of wine and relax, then go from there. If at any time you want to back out, then of course, we stop."

Zoe squeezed her knees together, as images of them filled her head. He was offering her a piece of what she'd wanted for so long. Only it didn't come with all the trimmings that she'd imagined in her fantasies of them. Should she take what he was offering and hope that they were so hot together in bed that he'd want more? Or would continuing on with Dana's plan be a better option? It had certainly gotten Dylan's attention in a short amount of time. But what if he washed his hands of the whole thing when she turned him down? Plus, she hadn't consciously saved herself for Dylan, but was there really not anyone else she'd rather experience sex with for the first time? He must be attracted to her at the very least to be suggesting such a thing. He had to get his flag up the pole, after all. Okay, so maybe some men were machines and could perform regardless, but she didn't think that was true of Dylan.

Unless . . . *What if this is a mercy fuck? How do I ask him that, or do I even want to know?* "Dylan—this isn't . . . You don't pity me or anything like that, do you? That isn't what this is about, is it?"

His stunned look told her all she needed to know. There wasn't a hint of discomfort or guilt in it. There was simply astonishment at her question, as if he'd never entertained such a notion. "Zoe . . . no. Hell no. I'm not some kind of charity sexual worker. You're special to me, but you're also a beautiful, desirable woman. Admittedly, I've been a little blind until recently, but I'm not suggesting this because I feel sorry for you. That thought never entered into the equation."

"Forget I said that," she tossed in hurriedly. She was embarrassed she'd even brought it up, but it was good to know that he hadn't been thinking such a thing.

Dylan glanced down at his watch, then rose to his feet. "I've got to get home and change for work. Think about what I've said today and we'll talk tonight. Want to order a pizza and watch a movie? We haven't spent much time together lately." When Zoe raised her brow, he added, "Well, other than the eight hours you were passed out on top of me last night. And even though that was memorable, it's not the same."

"That sounds good," Zoe agreed. She was ready to take a night off from play-dating anyway. Dana probably had her new ex, Mike, all set up to escort Zoe—the pretend lesbian—to another movie. Sadly, she couldn't even count on scoring a free meal from these outings. "I'll see you around seven." She followed Dylan to the door and stood silently as he opened it. He paused on the threshold and for a moment she was certain that he thought about kissing her. His eyes had gone to her mouth and there had been indecision along with something that resembled desire before he abruptly turned and took off down the hallway.

"See you later on," he tossed over his shoulder before entering the stairwell. Apparently he was in too much of a hurry to wait for the elevator. Zoe stepped back into her apartment, closing the door behind her. What a crazy morning it had been. Not only had she attacked Dylan on the sofa, but he'd also offered to have sex with her. When she'd agreed to this crazy plan with Dana, she never imagined this would happen within the first week. Sure, she'd hoped that he would finally see her as a woman and not one of the guys. Then maybe at some point, fall in love with her and suggest that they go shopping for a minivan. Nowhere in her fantasies had he offered to give her just one night of sex. She knew that she had an important, possibly life-altering choice to make. She'd talk to Dana and see what her opinion was as well. But at the end of the day, when all was said and done, she was pretty sure that her decision had already been made before Dylan finished asking the question.

~❀~

Dylan couldn't believe that he'd propositioned his best friend over breakfast. Okay, maybe he'd called it making love, but wasn't that splitting hairs? The idea had taken root in his head last night and then again this morning while he was gone for breakfast. But he'd planned to wait until she'd recovered sufficiently from the previous evening before talking to her. He didn't exactly regret mentioning it now, but certainly he could have approached the whole thing a bit more delicately. Zoe was a virgin and he'd said something like, "Hey baby, how 'bout I do you one night after McDonald's and a box of wine." *Smooth, Dylan, really smooth. Fuck, you're usually better than that.*

No wonder she hadn't been in a hurry to give him an answer. She was probably calling Paul right now and begging him to do her after Dana left for work. At the thought of the other man, Dylan's fists clenched. *Mine*, he thought. Shit, things were already getting confused in his head. He wasn't possessive of the women who came and went from his life. He wasn't with them long enough for that to be an issue. He couldn't care less if they were screwing someone else the next night. It was a few hours of pleasure, maybe more if he really needed to blow off some steam. He made it known up front that he wasn't looking for anything more than that. If that was a deal breaker, then he moved on—no big deal.

SYDNEY LANDON

But for all of his bravado earlier, he couldn't imagine just one night with Zoe. Sure, he could be wrong and the sex might be horrible and the whole situation unbearably awkward. After all, a week ago he wouldn't have imagined this scenario ever coming up. That was before his sensible Zoe had turned into hot Zoe. If she'd stayed in those damn khaki shorts and that polo shirt, he wouldn't be so confused. She'd gone and changed the game, though, and he'd been struggling to adjust ever since.

It wasn't that he was a man obsessed with appearances. Zoe had always been pretty to him, but in a safe kind of fashion. She dressed in a way that downplayed her physical attributes and made it easy for him to keep her firmly in the friend category. Sure, there had been cracks in his armor a few times through the years. Even her conservative one-piece swimsuit made him swallow uncomfortably, but then she'd pull a long, shapeless T-shirt over it and all would be right in his world again. He had a bad feeling that she didn't plan to return to the Zoe he'd always known. Which meant more dating, revealing clothes, and driving him insane.

Once he started thinking about being her first, though, he hadn't been able to get it out of his head. Maybe it was warped, but it seemed almost like a natural progression of their relationship. They'd been there for so many of each other's firsts. How was this any different? He knew that he could make it an amazing experience for her.

Tonight he'd talk to her again and try to smooth over the mess he'd made of things this morning. She was probably nervous about finally having sex, and he needed to set her at ease. A part of him couldn't believe he was thinking of going there with Zoe. What if it forever messed up their relationship? Could they go back to being buddies afterward? They had to; he couldn't live with anything less. A world where she wasn't a prominent part of his life wasn't acceptable.

Zoe would agree to his offer and he'd help her overcome any fears she might have before they enjoyed one night together. Then things would return to normal and he'd be able to focus on something other than her. A feeling of peace settled over him. He was in control and everything would fall right into line as it always did for him. No problem.

Seven

"Pardon?" Dana asked, blinking rapidly. "I thought you just said that Dylan wanted to punch your V-card for you. Please don't tell me I have that wrong."

"Nope, that's about it." Zoe smiled at the other woman's stunned expression. She'd felt that way herself earlier, but some of the shock had worn off over the last few hours and she could actually talk about it now without squealing like a teenager who just got asked to the prom.

"Holy shit," Dana hissed. "Apparently I missed some good stuff when I left last night. I didn't even think he knew you hadn't had sex. Man, you two really do tell each other everything, don't you?"

Zoe took a drink of her iced tea before saying, "Oh

no, he wasn't aware of it until I blurted it out at some point during the evening while I was sprawled on his chest in a drunken heap. I'm pretty sure it was before I stuck my tongue down his throat and tried to run my hands down his pants." They had walked next door to the Olive Garden for lunch and Zoe took a bite of her spaghetti while her friend struggled to process her words. Obviously the thought of her doing those brazen things to Dylan was boggling Dana's mind.

"You slut," she finally said, and laughed. An older couple at the next table gave them a glare of disapproval, but Dana just waved them off. "Whatever you did, it must have worked big time for him to make that offer. I didn't expect anything like this when we set out to get his attention. Heck, if that was all it took, you could have confessed your virginal status years ago—damn."

"I know, right?" Zoe mumbled around a breadstick. "Although it was kinda mortifying. I'm afraid he just feels sorry for me and is willing to take one for the friendship team."

"Yeah, right." Dana smirked. "Dylan is doing this because he wants to get in your pants now, plain and simple. Once he noticed that you were no longer one of the guys, he lost his flipping mind. And I'm sure he damn near had a stroke when you spilled your big secret to him. I'm betting there is no way he plans to let you sleep with another guy. He might not know it

yet, but he's falling for his best friend. If I had to haz-
ard a guess, I'd say he's felt the same way as you have,
he just wasn't smart enough to realize it. Damn, it's
amazing what some new boob-baring clothing and
competition will do to a man. You so need to burn that
old work uniform when you get home. That thing has
kept you a virgin for entirely too long."

"A good pair of khakis are timeless," Zoe protested.
"Lots of people wear them every day."

Shaking her head, Dana said, "Um, sure, but those
are mostly men, little old ladies, and women who've
given up on getting laid. In case you're wondering, you
were in that last category until recently."

"I hate to say this," Zoe admitted grudgingly, "but
you might have a small point. I haven't exactly had an
active social life these last few years. Wait"—she snapped
her fingers—"I'm forgetting all about Travis. We dated
for several months. He really liked my work clothes. He
called them 'charming.'"

Dana wrinkled her nose. "He was like forty and
still lived with his mother. Plus, didn't he end up mar-
rying his cousin after you two broke up?"

"I'm not sure," Zoe said evasively. "But I don't think
it was a super close relation. The point is, there have
been a few men."

"None you slept with, though," Dana pointed out.
"Whether you realized it or not, I think you were always
saving that for Dylan." Cringing, she added, "Geez, can

you imagine old Travis being your first? He'd probably have had to call his mommy first for permission to stay out past eight o'clock."

Zoe couldn't contain the giggle that bubbled out. "She didn't like for him to be out late on a work night, that's for sure." So Travis hadn't been exactly manly. He'd cried during the first movie they'd seen together and it had been a chick flick. She'd gotten in the habit of taking a purse full of tissues with them, not for her, but for him. And he'd been more than content to let her call the shots where the physical aspect of their relationship was concerned. He hadn't even kissed her until they'd been dating for a month. The fact that she hadn't cared spoke volumes about her feelings for him. Truthfully, she'd stayed with him for so long because it was easy. There was never any pressure to take things to the next level. It was companionship and she'd been able to tell others that she had a boyfriend. God knows it got old having to hear the inevitable, "Are you seeing anyone?" or "When are you going to settle down and get married?" Um, hello . . . it wasn't as if she was being too picky and fielding offers for her hand every day.

"So you are going to take advantage of this offer by Dylan, right? Hell, the man even tossed in dinner and booze. I've dropped my panties for far less."

"Of course I am," Zoe agreed without hesitation. "I'm just not sure how to go about it. He said we'd talk tonight, but I don't want to talk! Is it too much to ask for a little passion? It sounds like he's trying to schedule my car for a tune-up instead of, you know, tuning *me* up."

"I see your point," Dana mused. "But in one way, you should be grateful. At least you aren't likely to be caught with hairy legs and an untrimmed bush. You know, if you're not happy with what he's proposing, then take matters into your own hands. You really hold all the cards here. Dylan wants you; he wouldn't be doing this if he didn't. If a spontaneous night of hot sex is what you'd prefer, then make it happen. When he comes over tonight to talk, rip his clothes off instead."

Zoe stared at the other woman, thinking she was crazy, until it hit her. She liked what she was hearing. In her fantasies, wasn't that exactly how she dreamed it would be between them? She wanted for them both to be so turned on that nothing was scripted. They simply did what felt good. If her first time was on the living room floor or the kitchen table, then so be it. If this was the only night she'd ever have with Dylan, then she wanted it to be something neither of them would ever forget. And while making love in a bed like adults sounded terribly romantic, she'd trade it in for wild monkey sex any day. Hopefully if things went well, she'd have the opportunity to experience the other kind in the near future anyway. "You're absolutely right," she said, nodding. "I might not have very much experience, but I haven't read all of those smut novels for years without picking up a few things. I'm going to do it," she said excitedly. "Somehow I'm going to push him over the edge and show him what he's been missing all these years."

"Check, please," Dana called out to their waiter across the room. "We're going to Victoria's Secret. This calls for some lingerie. I swear if you even look at anything with the word 'cotton' on the label, I'll smack you." They quickly paid their check and got into Dana's SUV.

In twenty minutes they were standing outside a store that Zoe had avoided most of her adult life. She tended to buy her underwear in packs of three, which Dana swore broke most of the commandments of being a woman. "I don't know about this," she whispered to her friend as they walked in the store and were given an assessing look by a nearby salesclerk. "Walmart actually has some pretty nice things."

Dana rolled her eyes and grabbed her hand to pull her toward a display of the skimpiest panties Zoe had ever seen. "Now, this is what I'm talking about," she said, holding up a pair.

Zoe frowned as she studied the silky scrap of fabric. "It's nothing but a string," she pointed out. She'd only worn a thong one time and that had been more than enough. It had felt as if something was wedged in her crack all day. She'd heard of suffering for fashion, but that had been taking it too far. Plus, it wasn't as if anyone was looking at what she had on under her clothes. *I hope that's going to change tonight, though.*

"It has some extra material in the front," Dana pointed out. "And it has a gorgeous matching push-up bra. You're what, a C cup?" Before Zoe could answer, Dana held the bra up to her chest. "In this baby, you'll look like a D. Your man has already been staring at your chest, so obviously he's into tits."

"I'll take it," Zoe agreed quickly, snatching it from Dana's hands. "Actually, I'll get a few of them." She inwardly winced as she added several more pairs of the uncomfortable-looking panties. In case their one night turned into more, she needed to be prepared.

She turned and was heading in the direction of the register when Dana called out, "Not so fast there. No self-respecting woman comes in Vickie's and leaves in under five minutes. This is the first table we've stopped at." Waving a hand to encompass the other displays, she added, "We have more exploring to do. While I've got you in here, we're going to look at some work undies, some casual ones, and of course, naughty ones. Then we're going back to your place to burn your old ones. If I let you keep them, you'll fall right back into your homely habits."

"Bu-but some of them are still new," Zoe protested. "I can donate them to charity. Someone would appreciate them."

Dana wrinkled her nose. "I've seen you changing in your office before. Not even homeless people want those cast-offs, trust me."

By the time the shopping trip was over, Zoe had spent the equivalent of a house payment on lingerie that was likely to crawl up her ass and barely cover her nipples. Dana stood next to her smiling proudly as the clerk swiped her credit card after wrapping her purchases in tissue paper. Apparently, when you sprang for the good stuff, there was a whole process to bagging it. She'd bought china before that didn't get treated as well as a pair of twenty-five-dollar panties. She wanted to grab the bag and stuff everything inside, but was forced to wait as each piece received the same treatment. Even normally impatient Dana appeared riveted by the process. "I swear, I didn't think she would ever get finished," Zoe hissed when they made it back to the car. "I believe she was chanting some kind of special prayer for each set."

"Yeah, I heard that," Dana chuckled. "It sounded something like, 'May this finally get you fucked, amen.'"

"Oh, shut up." Zoe glared at her friend, then found herself laughing as well. "I better get something for the amount of money I just dropped in there."

"Honey, you've got what I call a golden beaver now. Men seem to know when you're wearing the good stuff. You'll have them trailing you in the coffee shop like a dog in heat."

"Thanks for that lovely mental image," Zoe cackled. "That would be a dream come true. But I'm only interested in one man, and I hope I have a chance to show him everything I bought today."

"Oh, you will," Dana said confidently. "I predict that after tonight, Dylan will be in your drawers every chance he gets. Seriously, though, don't be nervous, go with what feels natural. Dylan is experienced, so he'll make it good for you. I'd have a glass of wine before he gets there tonight to loosen up a bit and take care of the jitters."

Zoe did a thumbs-up before adding, "I've already got that planned. And strangely enough, I'm not completely freaked out. I'm more excited than anything. Whatever the reason, he's finally giving me the opening I've been looking for and I'm not going to miss the opportunity. If he wants to spank me, then I'm all for it."

"Damn straight," Dana boomed before saying, "Wait, do what? Spank you? Honey, he's not going to go all *Fifty Shades* on you the first time, and you probably shouldn't throw that out there as an option. I'm all for you letting it hang out, but hold off on the S and M until you've mastered good old-fashioned missionary. Dylan would probably swallow his tongue if you pulled some handcuffs and a belt out of your closet."

"Calm down, Mom," Zoe replied, giggling. "I was just using that for an example. I closed my eyes during that part of the movie, so it's not likely I'm going to ask him to redden my cheeks."

They were still laughing when they made it back to the coffee shop. Dana stepped behind the counter and began helping with the line that had formed. Even though it was hectic at times, customers equaled money, which was what every business owner needed to stay in the black. "There's my baby girl," a voice said from behind her.

Zoe whirled around, then grinned when she saw her mother standing there with her boyfriend, Marcus. "Hey, you two, I didn't know you were coming by." Friday nights were busy in the Oceanix restaurant and her mother normally chose to stay home and rest during the day before working the evening shift.

"I had some interviews for a new sous chef so Marcus came by to have coffee with me afterward. Great crowd in here," she added, looking around. "I bet my pastries are beginning to run low by now. I'll add some extra for tomorrow."

"Thanks, Mom, that would be awesome. We can't keep your special cinnamon rolls. I had a woman offer me her firstborn for a dozen yesterday."

"It's what keeps me hanging around," Marcus joked, before dropping a kiss onto her mother's forehead. Zoe had never known her father. He was a musician who had been passing through town back in her mother's "hippie life" as she referred to it. She'd missed having two parents at times, but her mother had filled both roles as well as she could. And when they'd come to the Oceanix all those years ago and she'd met Dylan, she thought she'd gained a brother, until her feelings had changed and he'd become so much more to her.

As if reading her thoughts, her mother asked, "Where's your shadow at?" Without waiting for a reply, she turned to Marcus, explaining, "You rarely see Zoe without Dylan. Those two have been inseparable since grade school. One day he's going to get a clue and figure out that she's the only one for him."

"Mom!" Zoe gasped out. "Someone's going to hear you." Her mother had always been firmly Team Dylan and had been vocal about her wish for Zoe to end up with him. Zoe had always downplayed it, not wanting to admit how much she wanted the same thing. She certainly wasn't going to tell her about the plan for tonight. Her mother would probably run out and buy her a case of condoms. She'd made her swear long ago not to say things to Dylan about hoping they'd become involved. She didn't want him to be uncomfortable around either of them or, worse yet, think Zoe had put her mother up to saying something to him.

"Well, a little push wouldn't hurt him," her mother grumbled. "I think he's sufficiently sowed his wild oats all over Pensacola."

"Let it go," Zoe scolded gently before giving her a hug. "I need to get back to work. Love you." Marcus embraced her as well before she walked away to help Dana. It seemed as if the only person in her life who didn't want her to end up with Dylan was the man himself. After tonight, she hoped they'd all be on the same page. She had hundreds of dollars of lingerie and a vague plan to help make that happen. If she had to go back to the drawing board afterward, she was afraid she'd throw in the towel and go back to her lonely way of life. Because Dylan was the only man who could bring color into her world, and without him, the most she could hope for were shades of khaki and stained polo shirts.

Dylan was uncharacteristically nervous as he stood outside Zoe's door. Hell, he'd been pacing the hallway for five solid minutes and was now late. He wiped his damp palms on his shorts and took another deep breath. She'd turned him into a basket case in the last few days. He hadn't been uptight about sleeping with a woman since he was a teenager. Now he was damn near having a panic attack at the thought of discussing it with his best friend. *Stop acting like such a pussy. This is Zoe.* Even as he tried to talk himself off a ledge, he couldn't escape the reality that wanting to have sex with her was messing with his head—both of them apparently.

He'd been useless at work again today. In a weak moment he even told his brother Asher about the whole thing. After the bastard had stopped laughing, he'd said it only confirmed what he'd been saying for years. That Zoe was the one for him. Otherwise, he wouldn't care that she was going to sleep with someone else. His brother just didn't understand the dynamics of their relationship, though, and Ash would be the first to admit that very thing. He didn't have women friends that he hadn't slept with. He said that blurred too many lines. His brother Seth, who ran the Oceanix in Myrtle Beach and had recently gotten married to his girlfriend, Mia, was the only one who'd ever halfway agreed that you could be friends with a woman without it involving sex. Dylan should have talked to him this morning instead of the man-whore brother. Ash's last words of wisdom were, "Get in and get out without putting a ring on it." Dylan didn't see himself married anytime soon, but he was fairly certain Ash would be a bachelor forever with his jaded views on relationships.

He was no closer to knocking on the door when the nearby elevator opened and the pizza delivery guy stepped out. Dylan recognized the kid and wasn't surprised when he stopped a few feet away. "Um . . . hey, Mr. Jackson, Ms. Hart ordered some pizzas." When Dylan made no move to open the door, the poor kid appeared at a loss for what to do. "Er . . . should I go ahead and knock? It's going to get cold if I keep standing here and I don't want to upset Ms. Hart."

Dylan fought the urge to roll his eyes. The little shit probably had the hots for Zoe and was disappointed to find him standing here instead. He pulled his wallet from his pocket and peeled off some bills before taking the boxes from his hand. "Thanks," he said abruptly, wanting the guy to go away before Zoe was alerted to his presence.

The kid's eyes widened as he took in the amount of the tip that he'd received. "Wow, thanks, bro." Dylan nodded, then inclined his head toward the elevator. *Can you fucking leave now? Shit.* Luckily, the kid got the hint and took off before Dylan put a foot on his ass and pushed him. *Now what?* he thought as he stood there with two large pizzas. This had gotten absurd. He needed to ring the bell and stop procrastinating. If Zoe seemed uncomfortable after their talk this morning, then he'd call the whole thing off. Tell her he was joking or something. Then he'd try his best to make sure she didn't sleep with some other guy. They'd drink too much wine like they usually did and have a big laugh over it. *Please let her be wearing the khakis*, he silently prayed as he finally reached out to ring the bell. Was it his imagination or did the damn thing sound like a gong of doom now?

When Zoe swung the door open, he swallowed his tongue, choked on it, then repeated the process another ten times while she grinned at him. "Hey, you, I was wondering where you are. You're never late. And why do you have pizza?" Looking past him, she added, "I've already ordered some."

Not the tight Daisy Duke shorts. Why, God, why would you do this to me? Fuck, she's braless too. Dylan coughed, attempting to clear the tightness from his throat before he croaked out, "He . . . I saw him on the way up . . . so . . . yeah, this is it." Her adorably confused expression told him that he wasn't making any sense so instead of explaining further, he extended the boxes and she automatically reached for them.

He followed behind her, which he figured out was a very bad idea when he couldn't remove his eyes from her ass. He missed plowing into her back by an inch when she stopped to set the food on the table. Why did she have to pick now to turn into a sexy little temptress? He'd be on blood pressure and anti-anxiety medication by the end of the month if she didn't start wearing more clothes. He tried to keep his expression blank as she turned to study him for a moment. Then her hand came out and touched his forehead. "You're all sweaty again, Dylan. I'm really getting worried about you. When was your last physical?"

He didn't even understand why he was suddenly sweating like a pig every time she was near. He'd be concerned too if it was happening at other times. He'd never had a reaction like this to a woman before. He might damn well combust if she got naked. The whole thing had gotten rather embarrassing. She probably wasn't interested in a man who couldn't form a coherent sentence and had buckets of water running off his forehead. What a turn-on. Maybe he should suggest that she buy a mattress cover. "We live in Florida," he joked, "have you noticed the humidity lately? Anyway, I'm starving, let's eat."

When he stepped around her and threw open one of the pizza boxes, she laughed. "Okay, think you can wait long enough for me to grab some plates?" Before she could get her question out, he had a piece stuffed in his mouth. "I guess not." She shook her head.

He knew he looked like a fool, but it had effectively distracted her and that's all he cared about. She went into the kitchen and came back with some plates, napkins, and a bottle of wine that appeared to be half empty. She pointed to her glass on the coffee table, saying, "I got started a little early, but there's more if we need it."

Dylan wished he'd thought of that. He could have caught a cab and had a few shots before leaving home instead of pacing her hallway like an idiot. No wonder she was so loose and relaxed. Sadly, that was a bad thing for him because he found her even more attractive now. Her cheeks were flushed and those full lips were ruby red. Her long, dark hair was casually tousled as if she'd run a hand through it countless times today. And those nipples, Jesus Christ, they were hard and pushing against the thin fabric of her white tank top. Where was she getting all of these form-fitting clothes? Damn, he missed the Sponge Bob lounge pants and the long Betty Boop T-shirt. "Let's have a seat," he mumbled around his pizza as he walked to the couch and lowered himself onto one end.

He almost jumped out of his skin when she sat down right beside him. There were barely a few inches separating their bodies. *No, no! This is all wrong. She always takes the other end. If she moves any closer, I'm going to be forced to fake a bathroom trip.* Luckily for him, they fell into their old routine of swapping funny stories from the coffee shop and the Oceanix. After three slices of pizza and two glasses of wine, he'd mellowed enough to relax. He'd also decided that he'd let a few days pass before bringing up his proposal from that morning. No use ruining the evening with any more tension. He had the television on and was flipping through the channels looking for a movie when she shocked the hell out of him by putting her hand on his leg. Everything ground to a halt as he zeroed in on her touch. It wasn't as if she was cupping his dick, but Zoe didn't sit this close when they hung out and she didn't cop a feel. *Don't make a big deal about it. She doesn't mean anything by it.* His voice sounded unnaturally high to his ears when he squeaked out, "Do you . . . um, see anything you like so far?"

His eyes flew to hers when she squeezed his leg. "I do." Then as if in slow motion, she licked her lips and his cock was in danger of becoming part of his zipper as it throbbed painfully.

This is all perfectly innocent. She's talking about a movie. This is all in your head. "I—which one? I'll flip back and you let me know when to stop." When she leaned over and took the remote from his hand, he was relieved. Thank God, he was right. Then she clicked the button to switch the television off and he froze. *Could have been an accident. You hit the wrong thing all the time on there. Don't assume.* "Do you not want to watch anything tonight? It has been a long week. I could probably use an early one myself."

He was on the verge of standing when the hand on his leg slid farther, stopping a few inches from his very eager cock. "I think going to bed now is a very good idea," she murmured.

If this was any other woman, he wouldn't be second-guessing himself. All the signs were there and he'd have to be blind not to pick up on them. But she was a virgin. Did she know what she was doing? *She's never acted this way toward you before.* Finally, he couldn't take it any longer. Fuck, he was a guy and thinking about shit like this wasn't his strong suit. He either clicked with a woman and things progressed from there or they didn't. It wasn't something that required this much thought. "Zoe, what are you doing?" he asked quietly. He didn't want to upset her, but he needed to know that they were on the same page here. He couldn't risk hurting or scaring her.

Even though her actions confirmed it, he was still

stunned when she answered without hesitation, "I want you, Dylan—now. I know I'm not very experienced with this, but surely you can see that."

And there it was, his heaven and hell. Attempting to be the voice of reason, he said, "We should . . . talk about this first. You might want to write down some questions you have." *I did not just say that shit.*

"You want me to take notes?" she asked in amazement. "Is that what people normally do, because they don't show this part in porn movies."

His mouth dropped open as he asked, "You watch porn? Since when?"

"You're sweating again," she pointed out. "Let me adjust the air conditioner."

"I don't give a shit about that," he snapped, "just answer my question."

Raising a brow in confusion, she said, "Well, of course I watch porn, doesn't everyone? I don't exactly have an active social life so I need something for, you know . . . inspiration. And even though I love reading romance books, the sex scenes in them don't come with pictures. Sometimes you really want the visual."

Dylan could only gape at her in disbelief. Who was this woman? They talked about everything, but she'd certainly never mentioned this before. Part of him was intrigued, but the other part wished she hadn't brought it up now either because he couldn't get it out of his head. He could so easily imagine her spread out naked on her bed touching herself while watching a dirty movie play out. *I'm going to die right here on this sofa. She's going to kill me saying stuff like that.* He had no idea how it happened or who made the first move, but one moment his heart was beating out of his chest and the next she was straddling his lap and her lips were fused with his. He groaned when their tongues came together in perfect sync. They'd kissed on her sofa, but he'd been half asleep and hadn't fully appreciated the sparks that sizzled when they touched. Hell, he'd thought he was dreaming when that happened and had freaked out and tossed her off him when he'd realized he wasn't. No way he was doing that this time, though. No. Fucking. Way. "Zoe," he growled as she dry-humped his lap. He'd never been this close to losing control before and they were still fully dressed.

His lips slid down her neck and onto the soft skin of her shoulder as his hands kneaded her incredible ass. "Mmm, feels so good," she purred as his hard cock rubbed against her core. They both needed fewer clothes on, immediately. He got shakily to his feet, still holding on to her. As he weaved his way toward her bedroom, her tongue licked the corner of his mouth before her teeth tugged on his lower lip. His knees damn near locked and he stumbled into a wall with a muffled apology. Luckily, he took the brunt of the hit and she only giggled and continued torturing him with her mouth.

Dylan's usual finesse in the bedroom seemed to be nonexistent as he loosened his grip for her to slide down his body. "Are you sure about this?" he asked one last time. He didn't want her to have any regrets in the morning. This wasn't quite the romantic evening he'd envisioned for her first time, but she certainly didn't appear to mind. She was more responsive than he could have imagined, which might well be his undoing. *God bless porn*, he thought when she put her hands on his stomach and began moving them lower. He was forced to stop her downward descent at the last minute, though, because he was afraid he'd blow his load early if she touched him there. He was barely hanging on from the sofa grinding.

She took a step back from him, which was a relief in a way. It gave him time to take a couple of breaths and regain his composure. That is, until she gripped the end of her top and lifted it over her head. *Holy. Fucking. Shit.* She was actually wearing a bra, he noted in surprise. Well, if you could call the filmy black scrap that. The thing had only one job and it did it well. Her tits were pushed together and appeared to be more than a handful. Why had he never realized how magnificent they were before? When her hands went to the button of her shorts, she paused and gave him a mischievous grin. "Wait, didn't you say something about taking notes?"

"Screw that," Dylan growled. "I don't think you

need any additional help, woman." With those words, he pounced. He'd like to say he was all smooth moves and experienced touches, but in truth they were both too eager to worry about skill. Instead, he peeled her shorts down, then sat back on his haunches to stare at her. Oh yeah, she had the matching panties on as well. Women didn't realize how much men loved that. There was something about a lingerie set that did it for him. "Absolutely beautiful," he hissed as he ran his finger up her calf.

It seemed a shame to remove the piece of lace, but he wanted to see all of her. With his eyes locked on hers, he slid the panties down her legs and she held his shoulder while she stepped out of them. His breath caught in his throat as he looked at the apex of her thighs. He could see her sex glistening through the neatly trimmed hair there. If he didn't taste her now, he'd lose his mind. Getting to his feet, he unhooked her bra and tossed it aside before pulling her against him for another mind-drugging kiss. Her skin was silky smooth beneath his palms as he memorized her shape and feel. "Oh, Dylan," she sighed into his mouth as he sucked the delicate skin below her ear. *This isn't high school; don't give her a hickey.* The urge to mark her was making him crazy and he had to wrench away before he let it happen. Shit, when was the last time he'd actually done something like that or even wanted to? Everything was different with Zoe.

He lowered her gently to the bed then positioned her on the edge. Her thighs parted and nirvana awaited. The scent of her arousal was all around him. The vivid image in his head of the first graze of his tongue through her folds was driving him insane. At the same time, his hands were shaking as the importance of the moment washed over him. He was crossing the friendship line with Zoe. Things would likely never be the same again, but even that jarring thought wasn't enough to give him pause. He wanted her more than he'd ever wanted anyone in his life. That realization alone gave him the strength to slow the pace. He wanted her first time to be perfect, and even if he died of blue balls right here on her bedroom floor, it would be worth it. She deserved the very best of him and he'd give it to her, no matter what the cost to himself.

～

Zoe discreetly pinched her thigh just to make sure she wasn't dreaming. *I can't believe I'm lying here naked in front of Dylan!* So far the whole experience had been amazing. There had been none of the shyness or awkwardness that she'd suffered from with other men. In fact, everything just felt right. Like they'd always been destined to end up here. As he got to his knees on the floor in front of her and pushed her thighs farther apart to gently wedge between them, Zoe thought she might die of bliss. Shouldn't she be freaking out right now? He was inches away from no-man's-land. Instead, her legs were like butter as he maneuvered them onto his shoulders. "Touch me," she whispered. That bit of encouragement seemed to be all he was waiting for as he lowered his head and she felt him lick her from top to bottom. Her body jolted as an electrical shock flew through her. *Sweet Jesus, how could I have missed out on this for so long?* Her toes were curling and she was making enough noise to wake the neighbors when he slid a thick finger into her wet heat. Like most women—especially the single ones—she had a vibrator, so it wasn't as if she'd never had anything inside her before. But it was a completely different feeling to have someone else in control of her pleasure.

"You're so tight, baby," Dylan growled out as if in pain. When she felt another digit join the first, she shifted uncomfortably against the full feeling. As if sensing her discomfort, he stilled his movements, letting her adjust. Then he sucked her throbbing clit into his mouth and she immediately forgot everything else. She could only focus on the fire racing through her veins as her orgasm came out of nowhere. "Let go, sweetheart—don't fight it," Dylan coaxed raggedly. Her world fell away, then came back in Technicolor as she shuddered around his fingers. Her body was so loose and wet by this point that she was barely aware of what was going on around her. She heard Dylan's husky laughter before he dropped a kiss on the inside of her thigh. "I take it you liked that."

"Mmmm-hmmm," she murmured. "What's next?" *Did I seriously just ask that question?* She'd have cringed, but she was simply too relaxed to care. *Does he expect me to return the favor now?* When he moved away, she struggled to sit up. Her eyes almost popped out of her head when she realized that he'd removed his clothes at some point and she'd missed it. *Holy big penis.* She couldn't help gawking at his size. He could give the guys in the porno movies a run for their money. When he started laughing, she realized she'd voiced her thoughts aloud.

"Thanks, sweetheart. I think I'll keep my day job, though." She felt her cheeks flush for a moment before curiosity got the better of her. "Can I . . . touch it?" she asked, unable to stop staring at his erect cock.

She almost swallowed her tongue when he fisted himself, shaking his dick lightly before pinching the tip. "Any other time, that would be great, but I'm too close to the edge right now and I really want to be inside of you when I come."

"That's so hot," she said fervently. Then she watched completely captivated as he pulled a condom from his wallet and proceeded to smooth it down over his long length. In what she hoped was an amusing display of eagerness, she scooted backward on the bed and waited for him to join her. If he had any doubts before that she was willing, he probably didn't now. She might as well be holding up a sign that read, COME AND GET IT. That was the beauty of experiencing this with Dylan, though. They'd been friends for so long that she didn't feel self-conscious. He knew she was slightly goofy and awkward about most everything in life. Why should sex be any different? And it certainly didn't appear to dampen his desire for her.

Then he was over her and settling his weight between her legs. His cock slid through the slickness at her opening before he pushed the tip inside. She braced her hands on his shoulders, tensing for the first time. "There's no way I can keep this from hurting, sweetheart, but I promise I'll go slow," he said as he looked at her tenderly. He lowered his head and took one of her nipples into his mouth, teasing the peak into stiffness before moving to the other one. Zoe's case of the jitters was gone as she moved restlessly against him. Then he was pushing inside her. Her breath caught as a twinge of discomfort threatened to pierce the haze of desire surrounding her. "I've got you, baby," he whispered against the shell of her ear as he stopped. "Let me know when you're ready to go on." She could feel his big body tremble as he fought to give her the time that she needed to adjust. The sting of pain was fading now and in its place was a fullness that demanded that she move. She shifted her hips warily and felt pleasure explode as his dick rubbed against her nerve endings. "Zoe," he groaned, but remained still, letting her experiment for another moment.

Zoe dug her hand into one of his butt cheeks and said, "I'm all ready to rock here." He chuckled before twining his fingers through hers. He began a series of shallow thrusts before she wrapped her legs around his hips and forced him deep. "Oh, Dylan, right there!" she cried out as he rubbed against a spot that had her seeing stars. Thank God the man had always taken direction well, because he continued to pound what she thought of as her magic button and within moments she was free-falling as the most powerful orgasm she'd ever experienced tore through her body. She screamed his name again and again as he increased his speed, causing her body to continually clench around his.

When he'd found his own release and collapsed on top of her, she could only stroke his sweaty back limply. She was so drained, she didn't know if she'd ever be able to leave the bed again. *How could I have waited twenty-nine years for this?* Simply put, sex was everything she'd never known she was missing. "How am I supposed to go back to a vibrator after that?" she asked idly. "You've ruined me for plastic, buddy."

Dylan's body began shaking against hers and she smiled when she realized he was laughing. She really could tell him anything. Not that she'd ever been this vocal about what she did in her alone time before, but what was the point in hiding it now? When a man had licked you intimately, embarrassment over little things seemed pretty silly. He rolled to his back as he continued to chuckle. "Are you expecting an apology for that?" he asked as he came up onto his side to grin down at her. Almost as if unaware that he was doing it, he reached out to stroke the tender skin of her stomach.

"Nope," she wheezed out, unable to believe that she could feel excited again so soon after being thoroughly sated. Which brought up the interesting question of "What now?" This was only supposed to be a one-time thing. So would he leave and then tomorrow they'd both act as if the whole thing had never happened? She darted a quick glance at him and noted that he appeared to be staring at his hand on her skin in utter fascination. She was struggling to come up with something to break the sudden silence that had fallen between them when her stomach took pity on her and growled loudly. Dylan jumped as if a bomb had gone off in the room. Rolling her eyes, she smirked, "Relax, that wasn't from the other end. Apparently, I'm a little hungry. I guess I worked up an appetite—you know, doing all the work just now."

And just like that the tension was broken. Dylan surprised her by leaning over to drop a kiss onto her mouth, followed by one on her nose and lastly her forehead. "I'll go warm the pizza." She stayed where she was and openly gawked at his fine ass as he strolled to the bathroom without a hint of embarrassment. She assumed he was discarding the condom and cleaning up. He was back a few moments later, pulling his boxers and shorts on while running his eyes lazily up and down her naked body. She could have pulled a sheet over herself, but again, why bother? He'd already been up close and personal. "Take your time, beautiful," he teased as he walked out of the room.

I'm so screwed. Zoe rolled over on her stomach for a moment, curling her arms around a pillow. Dammit, she should have known that Dylan would be just as good in the lover department as he was in friendship. He was gentle, patient, sexy, and dominant. He was prime rib. So how in the hell was she supposed to downgrade to hamburger? Not that it was really even an issue at this point. It wasn't as if she was seeing anyone else. There sure wasn't a line of men waiting to sleep with her. But still . . . at some point if she dedicated herself to actually having a social life, then the opportunity could arise. She was very much afraid that she'd compare every man from this moment on to her best friend.

Her rumbling stomach forced her from the bed. She took a quick shower then tossed on a sundress sans undergarments. He'd already seen it all, right? She laughed to herself, thinking she was using that rationale a lot now. But really, why bother with a ton of clothes? His T-shirt still lay across the bottom of her bed. She wanted to hide it so that she could keep it, but figured he might miss it when he went to leave.

Taking a deep breath, she prepared to enter uncharted territory. Was this the walk of shame? Wait—that was when you left a guy's apartment in the same clothes from the night before. At least she thought that was it. No, this was simply the slightly uncomfortable after-sex moments with your friend. She didn't want to make a big deal out of it, but if he punched her on the shoulder like he did occasionally, she'd probably kill him. *You've got this, girl. Just act casual, like you do this all the time.* Somehow, though, she felt like this next few minutes would set the tone for their relationship, and she only hoped that it was a step forward for them and not three back.

Eight

Dylan was seriously rattled as he slapped pizza onto two plates and shoved the first one in the microwave. He'd really done it. He'd slept with his best friend. The sex had been so hot that his dick was still hard. He wondered if the damn thing would ever go down again. Certainly not if she was anywhere in the vicinity. Hell, he wasn't sure how he'd work in his office during the day knowing she was in the same building. Visions of lunchtime quickies with her bent over his desk had him swearing under his breath. *Don't go there.*

Now he had no idea what came next. If she were any other woman, he'd already be gone by now. He didn't stick around afterward because it led to expectations.

But he simply couldn't take Zoe's virginity and then say, "Catch ya later." She was different from other women. He cared about her. Hell, he loved her like a sister—didn't he? Shit, that thinking was all wrong now that they'd slept with each other. He needed to admit to himself that his love for her was a different kind than that for family. He'd never taken the time to analyze it because men just didn't do that. In this one instance he wished that maybe he had at some point. He might not be this mixed up over the whole thing now.

This was only supposed to be a one-time thing. He'd been careful to make that clear, but now he wondered which one of them needed reminding, him or her. Because he was having a hard time accepting that she'd never been in his arms in that way again. Fuck, come to think of it, he wasn't even sure that they'd discussed the one-time thing that thoroughly. That part of it was supposed to have happened tonight, but, well . . . they'd gotten carried away. That made this even more uncomfortable. He didn't want to bring up something that would fuck this up, and truthfully, he thought he was possibly having a harder time letting go than she was. Maybe he'd just play things by ear and see what happened. She knew him better than anyone else. It wasn't as if she'd be picking out china and telling the hotel staff that they were an item. It was probably silly to worry about that at all.

He was still floored by how responsive she'd been.

And some of her questions and comments had been adorable. Despite it being her first time, she hadn't seemed nervous at all until he was sliding inside her. And that had only lasted a moment and then she'd relaxed and damn near killed him with her enthusiasm. She was quite simply every man's dream in bed. The jealousy roaring through him at that thought took him by surprise yet again. He'd hoped that those feelings were because he didn't want another man who didn't care about her like he did to be her first. But now the thoughts of her being the same way with anyone else made his stomach turn. The possessiveness was even worse now, not better. His heart kept insisting that she was his in every way while his mind was damn near in a panic. Never had he been so at war with himself over a woman.

This was a bad idea. You should have known better, you fool. What choice did he have, though? Let her sleep with some loser like Paul? Hell, knowing Dana, she would have probably joined them.

"Mmm, that smells so good," Zoe said from close behind him. He jumped, having been so lost in his thoughts that he hadn't heard her walk up. "Is sex like smoking pot? You know, getting the munchies and all that?"

A laugh burst out of him despite the anxiety that was threatening to weigh him down. She said the damnedest things. She always had, but now the topics included sex, which was rather unsettling, to hear her talk freely about her vibrator. *Down, boy. Don't think about that mental image.*

"It's been years since I've smoked weed, so it's hard to compare the two." He smirked. "Go ahead and take the plate in the microwave and I'll heat mine next." He realized too late that he should have shifted down some when she stretched past him to open the door of the microwave for her food. Her breast pressed against his arm and the smell of cherries filled his nostrils. His cock, which had subsided to half-mast, was now up and eager to go once again. He attempted to be discreet as he looked her way and saw that she was wearing a short sundress with tiny straps. There was no sign of a bra. Fuck, what about panties? Something told him she was completely bare underneath the thin fabric. She was so comfortable around him that it was torture. He needed her to bring the sloppy clothes back out. Where was the damned khaki when you needed it?

He quickly warmed his own food and took a seat at the table while she fixed them both a glass of Coke. He figured it was the safer option over the sofa. At least he thought so until she took the chair right beside him and settled in with her leg firmly against his. *You've sat this close a thousand times before. What's the difference? You're both wearing clothes.* Well, actually he hadn't bothered to put his shirt back on and suddenly he felt too exposed. *She's not going to lose control and attack you. Calm the fuck down.* "So . . . um, you wanna watch a movie next?" He had no idea why he was talking about prolonging the evening since he was a jittery wreck, but for some bizarre reason, he wasn't ready to leave either.

"Oh, yeah." She elbowed him. "We haven't seen that last Nicholas Sparks movie yet. It's on HBO Demand now."

"Ah, hell," he grumbled. "You know someone always dies in those and you cry for the last hour of the movie. Why do you do this to yourself time and again?"

"Hey, I caught you wiping your eyes the last time too. Don't even pretend that you don't like them," she teased. "I won't tell any of your macho brothers. It'll be our little secret."

"I'm pretty sure that Seth is doing the same shit with Mia now, so I'm not worried about it. On the other hand, if you tell Ash, I'll have to go into the witness protection program or something like it. He always gives me a hard enough time about you without knowing we watch chick flicks together. He'll automatically assume that we do each other's hair and nails as well."

"Poor baby," she mocked him. "Ash is rather intense, though. You know it's kind of strange that as long as you and I've been friends, I don't really know your brothers that well. I mean, of course I've spent time around them at company events, but shouldn't I be closer to them or something? Dana was so disappointed when she figured that out. She had this whole fantasy built up in her head about a Jackson brothers sandwich."

Dylan dropped his slice of pizza as he stared at Zoe. "You've got to be kidding. I'm telling you, sweetheart, she might be your friend and employee, but that girl has a screw loose somewhere. And for the record, that whole sandwich thing will never happen. Although I can't rule out one of my brothers having a lapse in judgment where she's concerned at some point in the future. I'm surprised they haven't already." He made a mental note to warn them away from her. They all had enough going on in their lives and didn't need to add any crazy to the mix.

They finished their food and then returned to the living room. As they usually did when they were watching a movie together, he took one end of the sofa and she the other. Dylan winced as the film started and he found himself drawn into the plot. His friends would laugh their asses off if they knew how many of these things he'd watched with her. Somehow, though, the routine felt off tonight after what they'd shared earlier. It wasn't that things were awkward between them because they weren't. Zoe hadn't even mentioned anything about them having sex. It was as if she'd accepted that it had happened and was content for things to return to normal. So why wasn't he? Because right now he wanted to pull her into his arms and do something totally mushy like watch this absurd movie with her head on his chest while he played with her hair. *You've completely lost it.* In some freak reversal of roles, Zoe appeared to be the guy and he the girl. Was he actually needing some kind of reassurance from her? A quick glance in her direction showed her riveted by what was happening on the television screen. She didn't look as if she had a care in the world. When her foot brushed against his leg, he could barely stifle a groan. Fuck, she turned him on. Even her innocent touches were sheer torture.

"There's no way she doesn't end up with the neighbor," Zoe whispered, bringing him out of the daze he had fallen into. "You can feel the chemistry between them whenever they're together. Her boyfriend doesn't stand a chance."

"So, um . . . you believe in that stuff. The whole instant attraction thing?" *What a lame-ass question. Why don't you go ahead and ask her if she feels that for you?*

She appeared to consider his question for a moment before nodding. "Sure, of course. I think we meet people who we're attracted to. Most of the time we don't act on it. It could be that they're married or involved or simply that we're not looking for anything right then. Instant chemistry doesn't equal sex or a relationship, but it's something you feel, like a little electrical charge."

Still fishing, although he had no idea why, he asked,

"So does that happen to you often? You meet a lot of people at work and a chunk of them are probably men. Ever felt the zap run through your system in that way?"

Zoe held his gaze for so long, he fought the urge to fidget in discomfort. Finally, she said, "Yeah, it's been there a few times through the years. I'm not sure the other person noticed the same thing, though, so it might not count."

Dylan knew they were on dangerous ground now. He wanted to ask her if she was talking about him, but why would she be? He'd engineered their night together. She hadn't confessed to any big attraction or crush on him. Now he found himself jealous of whoever she'd been drawn to. He wanted a name, address, and social security number so he could have the bastard investigated. He hoped to God the man was married with kids, a dog, and a mother-in-law who lived in full-time and kept an eye on him. "That's er . . . Yeah, that happens," he said lamely. "Was this one of your regulars?" *Please say no.*

"You could say that," she replied, while he ground his teeth together. At this rate he'd need dentures by the end of the night.

"Do you want to go to a party tomorrow night at Josh's?" he heard himself blurting out. He'd never asked her to one of his friends' parties because they tended to get out of hand at times. There was always an abundance of alcohol and women, so it didn't really make sense to bring a female buddy with you. Despite all of that, though, he wanted to spend more time with her. She'd met Josh and his other friends many times, so it wasn't as if she wouldn't know anyone.

"Wow, really?" she asked, sounding amazed. "I thought those were strictly a boys' thing."

Usually. "Nah, there'll be other women there. I thought you might enjoy it. There's going to be a really great local band playing that you'll like. And the food is amazing. It's casual, since we'll spend most of the time outdoors. You'd need to bring a swimsuit too. If it gets too hot, you'll want to cool off in the pool or the ocean."

"Sure," she said, looking a tad wary but pleased. "That sounds great. What time?"

"I'll pick you up around seven," he replied, feeling strangely excited at the prospect.

"Wait." She snapped her fingers. "I'm supposed to pick Mom's dog up from the groomer's at six and run her home. Can you give me the address and I'll meet you there? I'll take some clothes with me to change."

"Sure, babe, that works." They'd both turned back to the movie when it hit him—he was continuing to call her endearments as if it was the most natural thing in the world. Plus, he'd already basically asked her out on the universally accepted date night of the week. And he couldn't blame any of it on her because she'd been nothing but calm and cool. No pressure, apparently no damn expectations where he was concerned—nothing. He really needed to go home and regroup before he did something juvenile like asking her to go steady. She'd just lost her virginity after twenty-nine years; why was she so unaffected and why did he keep dwelling on it? He pretended to be engrossed in the drama of the on-screen couple but he couldn't escape the irony that he was starring in his own chick flick tonight, and damned if he wasn't the girl.

Nine

The coffee shop was always busy on Saturday, and today had been no exception. She'd barely had time to say two words to Dana, and curiosity was killing the other woman. Finally, around five, things quieted down enough for them to take a break. Dana made them both mocha frappes and herded Zoe to a secluded table in the corner. "I can't believe we've been here together for eight freaking hours and I'm just now getting to interrogate you about Dylan."

Zoe took a big sip of her frosty drink and sighed in appreciation. "Yeah, well, that was a good try with the note passing. Seriously, 'Did you do the nasty with Dylan? Check yes or no.' I almost dropped the latte I was working on when I read that."

"Hey, I was desperate. You were ignoring my texts. You know how nosey I am. This has been about to kill me. I swear to God if we'd had one more load of soccer moms with special orders, I'd have melted down right there behind the counter. 'Could I have a double shot with absolutely no fat in it but made with whole milk and whipped cream?'" Dana said in a perfect imitation of one of their waif-thin customers. "Dream on, sister. If we could invent that, Starbucks would be history."

Giggling, Zoe said, "I heard that and barely kept it together. She was totally serious too. Makes me wonder if she orders that somewhere else and they actually tell her they can do it."

Waving a hand, Dana said, "That's her problem. Now, did you get it on with Dylan last night or not? I thought you'd call me, but nada."

For the first time in her life, Zoe was in the kiss and tell position. Dana was always going into detail about her exploits in the bedroom, but since Zoe had never had sex, it hadn't been an issue for her. But now . . . it seemed rather wrong to share something so intimate with her friend. But she also felt she owed her. After all, without her help, it most likely wouldn't have happened at all. "We slept together," she admitted while toying with the straw in her cup.

"Mmmm, control your excitement over there; I can hardly stand it," Dana teased. "Did it suck? Oh shit, please tell me big Dylan wasn't actually little Dylan?

What is it with all the small dicks in Florida? It's like a pecker-demic or something. Did he at least know how to use it? You came, right?"

"It wasn't—no," she began before looking around and lowering her voice. "It was really . . . large. I know I don't have anything other than porn movies to compare it to, but it was right up there with the best ones I've seen."

Dana knocked her fist on the table. "Damn, I knew it! You can see the outline of that baby down his leg in some of those dress pants." Watching her intently, she asked, "So, it was good, right? You enjoyed it?"

"It was wonderful," Zoe admitted. "It was so much more than I could have even imagined. And I really wasn't nervous. We've been friends for so long that everything felt natural with him. I knew he wouldn't hurt me so I left everything in his hands."

"I'll bet you did, you tramp." Dana smirked before laying a hand on top of hers. "Seriously, though, sweetie, I'm thrilled for you. That was way past due to happen between you two." They sat in silence for another minute before Dana asked, "So, what happened afterward? Was it awkward? Did he run like his ass was on fire?"

"There were a few uncomfortable moments," Zoe admitted, nodding. "But then things kind of settled and we were more or less like we usually are together. I tried to be very casual about the whole thing so he wouldn't feel pressured because it was only supposed to be a one-time thing. I was surprised when he stayed for so long, though. I thought he'd leave just to prove some kind of point, like it was no big deal to him. But we ate pizza and watched a movie. At some point I must have fallen asleep because I woke up in my bed this morning and don't remember getting up and going there."

Looking curious, Dana asked, "Was there any cuddling during the film?"

"Nope, we were each in our own corners like always. He did call me 'sweetheart' and 'babe' some, though, which is different. I mean, he says stuff like that sometimes, but not often. And he invited me to go to a party with him tonight, which he *never* does. And it's at some guy's house, one of his single friends."

"No shit," Dana mused. "That's major player ground right there and he's bringing you, which means he has no plans to hook up with anyone else right away. Plus, he's also taking you around his boys. That's big, Zoe. I'm kinda impressed with Dylan right now."

Leaning her elbows on the table, Zoe asked, "Do you really think it means something? I was surprised when he asked because he's never even hinted that I was welcome at any of the parties he attends unless they're sponsored by the hotel. I've met most of his friends, but he keeps us separate for the most part."

"That's because you're his good girl and he wants

things a certain way with you. When he's with the guys, he's one of them and probably doesn't want you to see some of the shit they all get into. I think Dylan likes that you view him in a certain way, which is why it's kind of a major move for him to take you tonight. Unless he knows for sure that this is a PG-13 evening."

"He said there would be a band and food. I'm also supposed to bring a swimsuit. I need to run home and pack a bag since I have to pick up Dolly for Mom first."

Dana's eyes got big as she started frantically shaking her head. "Please, God, tell me you've bought a new swimsuit. You absolutely cannot wear that granny one-piece."

"What's wrong with it?" Zoe asked defensively. "Lots of people wear one-piece suits. They're in style now."

"It has big chlorine streaks all over it," Dana hissed. "Also—and I say this in the nicest way possible—it makes your butt look like a pancake. Friends don't let friends go out in something like that. You have Dylan's attention now, so let's not screw this up." Getting to her feet, she snapped, "Come on. Macy can watch things while we go to the hotel boutique. I know it's a bit expensive but Dylan gives you the employee discount and this is an emergency. If we don't buy one here, you'll stop at Kmart or Walmart and I can't have that. Now move!"

Zoe knew that it was useless to argue with Dana when she was in dictator mode. And truthfully, she had been meaning to replace the swimsuit. She'd had it for at least five years and regular swimming in her condominium pool had really done a number on it. "Oh, all right," she grumbled, "but I'm not getting some Kim Kardashian number."

"Honey, you don't have that much boobs or ass, so not a problem. We'll find you something to make the most of what you do have, though." They both grabbed their purses from the office and were soon crossing the luxurious lobby of the Oceanix. One wing of the resort housed exclusive shops that Zoe had rarely ventured into. Luckily, there was an entire boutique filled with nothing but swim apparel for the entire family. Apparently people actually visited the beach without coming fully prepared.

Dana shot inside the double doors like a hurricane and the salesclerk's eyes widened as she began pulling hangers from the racks and piling them in Zoe's arms. "They're going to call security," Zoe hissed as she attempted to give the clerk a reassuring smile. She knew a lot of the resort's employees, but unfortunately this wasn't one of them. "I own the coffee shop in the lobby," she offered in way of explanation. "My friend was just helping me pick out a swimsuit for tonight."

"She's going out with Dylan. You know, the owner," Dana called out. Suddenly the woman seemed to be looking at Zoe in a whole different light. Gone was the slightly panicked look and in its place was one of nervous respect. Zoe thought it had little to do with the coffee shop and everything to do with Dylan.

"Did you have to say that?" she muttered under her breath to Dana. "Now she's going to tell everyone and it'll get back to Dylan."

Dana rolled her eyes as she continued to pile on suits. "It's the truth. I was just trying to set her at ease. I figured she was going to push that button behind the counter anytime, and that would be even more embarrassing to you. Plus, you know they'll only let regular people carry back three pieces at a time, which would mean we'd be here for hours."

Zoe took a look at her watch and knew she needed to leave in thirty minutes or Dolly would be spending another night at the groomer's, which wouldn't make her mother happy. "All right, good point," she conceded as they were waved toward a fitting room. Dana stepped inside the spacious room first and hung up all the swimsuits. "Good grief, look at all of these mirrors," Zoe murmured uncomfortably. "They certainly want to make sure you can see every little dimple, don't they?"

"I doubt the women who shop here are worried about that kind of thing," Dana quipped. "Now, let's get moving."

Zoe pointed to the door, saying sternly, "You're waiting out there. I already feel self-conscious in here so I need to pretend I have a little privacy."

Giving a long-suffering sigh, Dana conceded. "Geez, okay. But you're going to show me all of them so I can help you make a decision." When Zoe reluctantly agreed, the other woman stepped out and took a chair in the small seating area.

Zoe quickly undressed, trying not to look at the mirrors before picking up the first hanger. Then the next . . . and the next. "All of these are two-piece," she called out. "Where are the one-piece?"

"Um . . . on the rack where they belong," Dana called out. "You've got a rocking body, my friend. It's time to stop hiding it behind granny gear. I promise you that Dylan will be attached to you at the hip all evening if you wear one of those." Zoe eyed the stack warily before finally putting on the first one. Then an amazing thing happened. She actually liked what she saw reflected back at her. Sure, she felt the urge to cross her arms over her chest in some of the more daring ones, but most of them were incredibly flattering. She actually looked thinner than she did in her old suit.

"That's the one!" Dana jumped up and down in excitement. "You look so flipping hot, I'm tempted to ask you out." Zoe studied her reflection and had to admit she looked good. There was so much skin showing, though. The black string bikini covered all the essentials and made everything in the surrounding area look better. She would have never dared wear anything like this before, but she was shocked to find that she was actually considering it now.

"I can't just walk around in this all night," she whispered uncertainly. "I like it, but I feel . . . naked."

"That's kind of the point." Dana grinned. "But we can get you a matching cover-up. Something sheer so that the suit isn't completely hidden, but you aren't so exposed when you're not in the water."

"This is going to cost me a fortune," Zoe grumbled as she shooed Dana back out of the room.

"There's no way you've been breaking the bank on the stuff you were wearing," Dana yelled through the door. "Think of this as a long overdue investment in your future."

Zoe rolled her eyes as she re-dressed. She expected a call most any day from her credit card company asking if her card had been stolen. Thank God for the generous discount the hotel gave their employees— and her. Otherwise there was no way she'd be able to bring herself to spend this much on a swimsuit, even if it did make her feel oh so sexy. She couldn't wait to see Dylan's reaction. If he didn't notice it, she was going to be so disappointed. This sudden need to impress a man seemed about ten years too late to her. But she couldn't argue with the results so far. And if a bikini would keep whatever she had with Dylan going, then she would gladly pull her Visa out and splurge yet again. She had no idea what to expect tonight, but if she had anything to say about it, she wouldn't be going home alone.

⌒⌐

Dylan had arrived at Josh's house early to help set up the barbecue. It was close to seven when Zoe texted to let him know that she'd arrived. He'd suggested that she do that so they wouldn't spend time trying to find each other. He also thought she might be a little nervous about being around so many people she didn't know without him by her side.

He'd spent the day running errands and catching up on some work before coming to his friend's house. He'd had to talk himself out of dropping by the shop to see her. Damn, he'd wanted to so very badly. They needed time, though, to get back on their familiar friendship ground, and following her around like a puppy dog wasn't going to allow that to happen. *Why'd you invite her tonight, then?* Yeah, he still didn't have a good answer to that one. He'd felt an overwhelming urge to spend the evening with her and had already committed to this party. Seemed harmless enough at the time.

Thoughts of his night with Zoe had been almost impossible to cut off. No matter how many pep talks he gave himself, he couldn't stop them. Hell, he'd jacked off twice today already, which was highly unusual for him. Every guy made use of his hand on a

140

fairly regular basis. Sometimes you just wanted the simplicity of rubbing one out. But it wasn't usually that often, at least not for him. His last session was right before he left home. He figured if he took the edge off, he wasn't likely to get a fucking boner as soon as she was near.

At least that was his plan until he stood in the doorway watching her walk up the sidewalk toward him. *I'm fucked—totally fucked.* Her legs looked impossibly long as she approached him with a smile on her face. She was wearing skimpy jean shorts and some kind of sheer top—wait, was that her bra? Upon closer inspection and since his eyes were now glued to her tits, she appeared to be wearing a bathing suit top with a filmy excuse for a shirt over it. She looked smoking hot, and despite his two earlier hand-to-gland sessions, he was hard as stone. Thank God he'd worn his loose swim trunks, although he didn't think they concealed nearly enough. Swallowing audibly, he croaked out, "Um . . . wow, you look—good." *That's putting it mildly.*

She reached out to touch his arm and it went straight to his dick. *Sweet Jesus, down, boy.* He silently begged his wayward body part to behave before everyone at the party labeled him as a pervert. "Thanks," she replied, looking pleased by his compliment despite his shaky delivery. "This place is packed. I had to park down the street."

"Josh throws a hell of a party. You hungry?" he

asked and promptly wanted to groan when she licked those plump lips.

"Starving. The shop was so busy today, we worked through lunch. Something smells amazing."

Without thinking, he took her hand and threaded their fingers together as he pulled her inside. "Let's get you something to eat, then." *And maybe a blanket to cover up with.* Soon his smile was replaced with a frown as he caught sight of countless guys ogling her when she walked by. His narrowed his eyes and tightened his grip on her, silently making it known that she wasn't available. He knew a big majority of the men here and none of them were good enough for Zoe. She was far too innocent to handle what some of these assholes were into. Shit, she really needed more clothes on. *What was she thinking?* No sooner had that thought occurred than he realized she looked like most of the other women around them. He might not like it, but this was a pool/beach party and her attire was the accepted norm for this type of event.

They reached the grill, where Josh was expertly flipping burgers. The other man motioned to the nearby cooler of beer and Dylan pulled one out and handed it to him. Josh nodded his head in thanks before noticing Zoe standing next to him. His friend's mouth dropped open as his eyes tracked down her scantily clad form, then back up again. Dylan glared, feeling his jaw twitch. *I'm going to kill the bastard.* He saw the exact moment that he recognized her. There was shock, then interest. *No way, fucker.* "Zoe? Babe, you look absolutely amazing. It's great to see you. Come on over here and give me a hug. It's been too long." *Is he kidding me right now?*

Dylan was seething as Zoe, seeming to think nothing of Josh's enthusiastic greeting, stepped forward, and was immediately engulfed in an embrace that went on for far too long. "Thanks for having me," he heard Zoe murmur against the other man's chest. No doubt dirty thoughts were flying through his friend's head before Dylan managed to pull her back. He put his arm around her, anchoring her to his side to keep the same shit from happening again. Josh didn't miss the possessive move on his part and shot him a questioning look.

He shook his head and gave Zoe a squeeze. "Let's get you some food, sweetheart." They went through the buffet-style line and loaded their plates down before finding room at one of the nearby tables. He'd taken a few bites and was beginning to relax when a guy's worst hell happened to him. Not one, but two of the women that he'd slept with in recent months took the vacant seats on his other side. *Fuck, what else tonight?* Normally that wouldn't really bother him, but after having sex with Zoe, it seemed beyond awkward. And unfortunately Carey and Kristen were usually very vocal and flirty. He'd be on pins and needles wondering what would come out of their mouths. Maybe he could hurry this meal along and get Zoe away before any harm was done. "It's really hot out here, isn't it? If you'll finish up, we can take a dip in the ocean. Sound good?"

Before Zoe could answer, Carey draped an arm on his shoulder as she pushed her huge tits against his arm. "I certainly need to cool off. I'm literally overheating for some reason." *For the love of all that's holy.*

"I'd love to take the plunge with you and Carey," Kristen purred as she winked at him. She might as well be holding a billboard, because her meaning couldn't be clearer. Dammit, he knew he'd regret that one crazy night with both of them. That was something he didn't want Zoe knowing about.

When he finally worked up the nerve to glance over in her direction, she was staring down at her hamburger as if it held the secrets to world peace. *She knows. Shit!* How could she possibly not? Ignoring the others, he nudged his knee against Zoe's and asked quietly, "Food okay, honey?"

She looked up, giving him a forced smile before saying, "Sure, it's great." She tugged on the hem of her shirt as if suddenly self-conscious about what she was wearing. He'd never regretted the way that he lived his life before, but in this moment, he was more than a little embarrassed. Zoe had met different women who he'd hooked up with before. It had always been a standing joke between them. She called them his "bimbo of the night." Ironically, Carey and Kristen seemed to fit that description perfectly.

"Hey, Dylan." Carey tugged on his sleeve. "Why don't we get out of here? Maybe go back to your place like last time."

"That was amazing," Kristen piped in, "and your apartment is freaking amazeballs."

Shoot. Me. Now. Dylan closed his eyes for a moment while he attempted to regroup. He had to get them away from the two idiots before this got even worse. Did these women have absolutely no class? For all they knew, he could be here with his girlfriend. Wasn't it obvious that he and Zoe were together? Hell, they'd probably invite her to join in next. Zoe took the matter out of his hands when she got abruptly to her feet. "I'm going to go for that swim now. You, um . . . have a good time." Before he could stop her, she was striding across the sand.

He stood, intent on following her, but turned to the women remaining at the table before he left. "Listen, ladies, we had fun together, but that's over. I'd be very grateful if you wouldn't mention it again, as it's upsetting to my . . . er, Zoe."

Carey and Kristen both appeared stunned by his speech. Hell, maybe he was a tad bit as well. But he didn't want them following after him and spewing more sexually laced invitations. "Are you, like, married or something now?" Carey asked, clearly not thinking that could even be possible.

Impatient, he put his hands on his hips and shook his head. "No, I'm not. It's . . . kind of complicated. But I'd really appreciate it if you'd cool it with flirting."

Without waiting for an answer, he gathered their empty plates and tossed them in the trash before going after Zoe. There were several other people already in the water, so it took him a few minutes to locate her. He'd expected her to be alone, so he was surprised to see that she was standing waist deep talking to fucking Josh. How had his friend even managed to get away from the grill and in the ocean in such a short amount of time? Apparently a skimpy swimsuit was just the right motivation for him. Zoe appeared relaxed again now and completely clueless to the fact that Josh had his eyes plastered to her chest where the outline of her nipples were clearly visible through the wet material. "Aren't you supposed to be cooking?" he snapped at the other man as he made his way to Zoe's side.

Giving him an amused smirk, Josh said, "I had Craig take over for a while. I felt a sudden need to cool off and I ran into your lovely best *friend*, so it's my lucky day."

Dylan didn't miss the emphasis he put on the friend part. What kind of game was the bastard playing at? He was deliberately baiting him and he had no idea why. He'd always liked Josh; he was one of his closer friends. But Dylan also knew that the other man was a major player, and if he thought Dylan would allow him to try something with Zoe, then he was sadly mistaken. As soon as he could get him alone, he'd set him straight. "Isn't that nice," he managed to get out while attempting something approaching a smile.

Josh looked like he was fighting back laughter while Zoe gave him a questioning look before asking sweetly, "Where'd your friends Candy and Mandy go?"

"I think you mean Carey and Kristen, and I have no idea. We're not friends. I barely even know them." That much was technically true. He'd learned long ago you could sleep with a woman without knowing all the intimate details of her life.

Both Dylan and Zoe turned to stare at Josh as he started laughing. "Man, that must have been awkward as hell for you, bro," he gasped out. Dylan pinched the bridge of his nose as he attempted to control his temper. He was struggling to deal with emotions that he'd never experienced before and he didn't mind admitting that he was confused and agitated. As he stood there wishing he could close his eyes and end up in some alternate reality, he had to wonder if his life would ever be the same again.

⁓

Despite her earlier anger at Dylan and his bimbos, Zoe found herself feeling sorry for him as Josh continued to antagonize him. She had no idea what was going on between them because they'd been friends for years. The other man had never paid much attention to her when their paths crossed. He was polite, but that was about it. Today, though, no doubt thanks to her new swimsuit, he appeared to be fascinated with her. She couldn't take all the credit, though. She thought that he also simply enjoyed riling Dylan up, which pissed her off.

Carey and Kristen had been a bad reminder of the type of women that Dylan usually went for. They were gorgeous, eager to please, and up for anything. She'd joked with him for years about that very thing and it hadn't bothered her that much when they weren't sitting inches away fawning all over him. It did give her some comfort that he didn't appear to be returning any of their affections. In fact, he looked distinctly uncomfortable with the whole thing and he followed after her within moments of her storming off. Unfortunately for them both, though, Josh had been right on her heels when she'd walked into the water and his eyes had barely left her chest since then. She really wasn't used to this type of overt male appreciation, and it left her wanting to cross her arms and turn away. She'd made the mistake of submerging her upper body before Dylan arrived and now the tiny top was almost X-rated. *Why did I let Dana talk me into this one? I could have gotten another nice, conservative one-piece.*

The tension surrounding them was thick enough to

cut with a knife. Tired of being the star of whatever spat these two were engaging in, Zoe turned and tossed over her shoulder, "I'm going for a swim. I'll see you later." Not bothering to wait for a response, she dove into the water and swam as far as she could before surfacing. She didn't look back; instead she settled into a leisurely swim and felt the weight of the last few minutes fall away as she enjoyed the tranquility of the ocean.

She wasn't sure how far she'd traveled when she flipped onto her back before promptly letting out a scream. Dylan was doing the same thing inches away. How had she not heard him swimming that closely to her? "Take it easy," he murmured as she flailed about in the water for a moment before settling down.

"You scared me to death," she hissed. "Where did you even come from? I thought you were still with Josh." Looking around, she added, "God, he's not out here somewhere, is he?" She looked down as if expecting him to come up from underneath her at any time. She doubted he was above swimming underwater to check out her bottom half.

Dylan had his eyes closed as if his early tension had never existed. "Nope, he went back to the house to be the host. It wasn't much fun to torture me after you'd gone so he gave up pretty easily. Thanks for that, by the way. My hands would probably be around his neck by now if you hadn't taken off."

Moving over to float side by side with him, she

asked curiously, "So what's the deal with that? He's one of your best friends, right?"

"He is," Dylan agreed. "But he can get a little cocky at times, especially if he thinks he's getting under my skin."

"That's what I'm not clear on. You two seemed to be having some silent battle. I felt like I was the only one of us not getting it."

Dylan remained silent for so long that she thought he wasn't going to answer and she'd decided not to press the issue when he said quietly, "I didn't like the way he was looking at you. You're right, we are friends and have been for a long time, but you and I are closer. I know I'm not a saint—far from it—but Josh makes me look good. This is a tame evening for him. Generally, his parties are far worse. He's into some weird shit, and trust me, you don't want any part of it."

Attempting to keep her voice level, Zoe asked, "Have you ever . . . you know, shared someone with him?" She squeaked in alarm when he promptly disappeared underneath the surface in a flurry of flailing limbs. "Dylan!" She had taken a deep breath and was going after him when his head popped out of the water. Apparently he'd ingested a mouthful of water at some point because he was coughing and sputtering. "Are you all right?" she asked as she moved over to pat his back. Dylan was a strong swimmer so she'd never seen the ocean get the best of him.

"Fine," he choked out. "You . . . um . . . kind of broke my concentration for a moment with that question."

She wrinkled her nose, trying to remember what they were talking about, then it hit her. "Ohhh, you mean the sharing one. I guess you don't need to answer it. If it was enough to make you almost drown, I'm pretty sure I can figure it out for myself," she added dryly.

"Let's swim back in some," he suggested. Motioning her ahead of him, she reluctantly retraced their earlier path until she was able to stand with the water just past her chest. She felt his hand on her back as he came up next to her. She was surprised that instead of putting some distance between them, he turned her until they were facing each other, then pulled her loosely into his arms. Her nipples immediately turned to stone as they nestled against his muscular body. He dropped a kiss onto her forehead before saying, "You know I'm not a saint, sweetheart, nor have I ever claimed to be."

You have no right to be jealous. Don't let him see that it bothers you. "I was just kidding, Dylan. Lighten up," she joked as she attempted to pull away.

She froze in place, forgetting all about putting distance between them when he admitted softly, "I don't know what we're doing. I'm totally confused about us. I know I'm sending mixed signals because even I recognize them. It's just that . . . things are supposed to be one way, but the lines are blurring." Looking at her intently, he asked, "Please say you're having the same issues; otherwise I'm going to pretend I never said what I did."

Zoe laid her head against his chest, comforted by the steady beat of his heart beneath her ear. "I'm with you," she confessed. There was no way she could tell him that she'd had those types of feelings for him for years. He wasn't ready to hear that. She didn't want him to feel as if she orchestrated this whole thing to get his attention, even though she had. She'd done it out of love, though, and not some need to trap him.

He breathed what sounded like a sigh of relief before saying, "Thank God, because that was going to be awkward as hell. I know we were only supposed to be a one-time thing, but I'm having trouble separating my friend from my lover. In my mind now, you're both and . . . I like it. I've never been a relationship guy. I work too much for a woman not to feel neglected after a while. Shit, I'm not even sure what I'm proposing here. I guess what I'm trying to say and making a mess of it is that I'd like to see what this is between us. Even suggesting this scares the hell out of me because I don't want to lose you if things don't work out in that way between us."

"That'll never happen," Zoe assured him as she ran a hand up and down his back soothingly. "I can't imagine my life without you in it. We don't have to make a big deal out of this. I'm attracted to you in a way that goes beyond simple friendship and I think you're saying that you are as well." When he nodded in agreement, she added, "Then how about we take each day as it comes? I know you spend a lot of time at the office and you know I live at the shop some days. It's who we are. We've always made time for each other and I say we continue to do that. Only maybe in a more romantic way than we normally would. Does that make sense?"

"Yeah, baby, it's perfect." Dylan grinned before slowly lowering his head and taking her lips with his. His tongue teased and plundered her mouth, while he slid his hands under her ass and pulled her against him until she wrapped her legs around his waist. "Fuck, you feel so good," he groaned as she ground herself against his rapidly hardening length.

Zoe lost all awareness of time and place as they swayed with the currents while devouring each other. She had no idea how he'd even managed it but somehow her nipple was in Dylan's mouth and he was sucking and biting the sensitive peak until she was on the verge of coming from that alone. "Dylan . . . I need," she gasped out as he kept one hand on her ass to hold her in place and wedged the other one between them, sliding it inside her bikini bottoms. She whimpered as he touched the bundle of nerves there, nearly sending her into orbit. "So good," she cried as she rode his hand. She was mindless to anything but the mounting tension in her body as she sought release.

"That's it, sweetheart," Dylan growled as she began shaking. The pressure that had built to an almost unbearable level suddenly broke and she was spiraling out of control. "You're so beautiful," she heard him say as she shamelessly took her pleasure. When she collapsed limply against him, he removed his hand and held her tightly for a few moments as her breathing calmed and she returned to her senses.

"Oh my God." She stiffened abruptly before raising her head to glance around. There were several people in the water around them, but luckily no one appeared to be paying them any attention. "I can't believe we did that out here in front of everyone. Do you think any of them knew what we were up to?"

Appearing thoughtful, he said, "I don't know, babe. You were really loud. Especially when you were yelling, 'Harder, harder!' I thought I noticed a few people looking in our direction then, but I can't be sure."

"Shit!" she hissed. "I'm like one of your bimbos now. What's next, us fornicating in the lobby of the Oceanix while my mother is walking by? Maybe having a foursome with Dana and Paul while he says, 'S'up.'" She pinched his arm when she felt his big body shaking in laughter against her. "It's not funny. I've never been a slut before. But now I'm the one that people will call the 'tidal tramp' or something catchy like that."

"I was only joking," Dylan managed to get out between fits of laughter. "To my knowledge, no one is any the wiser that I had my hand in your pants. We were kissing most of the time so I pretty much swallowed the majority of those sexy little moans you were making. And if anyone did hear, then they're not talking trash about you. They're jealous because they either weren't the one with you in their arms or they weren't the one getting finger-fucked so good that the rest of the world ceased to exist."

"I hate you." She pouted, then squealed as his arm suddenly left her bottom and she tumbled into the ocean. She was only under for a second before he was pulling her back out again. "You ass!" she sputtered as she wiped the water from her face.

"Now, now," he teased, "that mouth was what got you dunked in the first place. If you're not a good girl, it's going to happen again."

Doing her best to look contrite, she said, "I'm sorry. You know I didn't mean it." And of course, as she'd expected, he fell for it hook, line, and sinker. So the last thing he was expecting was for her to stick her leg between his and wrap her foot around his calf before pulling with all her strength. He went backward with impressive speed, hitting the surface with a huge splash. Instead of helping him up, though, she crossed her arms over her chest and waited for him with a huge grin on her face.

They played for at least an hour, each trying to best

the other before fatigue finally drove them back to the shore. Zoe couldn't help laughing as they approached the buffet tables for another plate and she saw Carey and Kristen snuggled up to Josh. She wasn't surprised at all that they were very much the "love the one you're with" type of girls. Josh had the good grace to give her a sheepish grin before pushing his fist out to bump Dylan's. It appeared that the earlier discord between the two friends had disappeared for the moment. Zoe was also glad that he no longer appeared to be trying to see through her clothes. While it had been flattering at first, it had quickly just turned uncomfortable. The only man she wanted admiring her assets was the one with his arm curled around her waist while they consumed hot dogs and beer. When they were finished, Dylan said a round of good-byes to his friends and led her toward the driveway. "I'll leave my car here tonight and drive us home in yours. It's late and I don't want you traveling alone. Plus, you've had alcohol and you know that goes straight to your head."

"You had a beer too," she pointed out.

"Honey, I'm a two-hundred-pound man. That's the equivalent of pouring a cup of water over my head. I'd need to have a helluva lot more than that. And trust me, if I was impaired in any way, I'd never get behind the wheel of a car with you."

Awww. Zoe felt her heart melt a little at his words

and the fact that he dropped a kiss onto the top of her hand at the end of it. For a man who'd banged his way through the state of Florida, he could be surprisingly sweet at times. As they walked down the street to where she'd parked, she fought the urge to pinch herself to see if she was dreaming. They were really doing this. Well . . . they weren't actually calling it a relationship, but they were pursuing more, which was better than she'd hoped for at this early stage. Naturally, in her fantasies he'd spend a few weeks feeling miserable until he realized that he needed her as more than a friend. She couldn't believe he'd actually brought up the subject tonight, just twenty-four hours after they'd slept together. Dana was absolutely going to be blown away; she certainly was. The fact that he was still concerned for their friendship was also a relief because that was her one fear about becoming involved with him. He'd been a part of her life for so long that she couldn't fathom a future without him in it in some form. She knew they were taking an awfully big risk by changing the dynamics of their relationship, but if she was right about him being the one man for her, wasn't it worth the gamble? As long as they both were committed to not letting anything come between them, then surely they would be okay either way—they had to be. Because she'd come too far to back away now. She was betting everything that they could be friends, lovers, and partners for life. *God, please don't let me be wrong about this*, Zoe silently prayed as she followed Dylan down the dark road, having faith that they would get to where they were going in more ways than one.

Ten

Dylan was cranky as hell when he got to the office on Monday morning. He hadn't seen Zoe since he dropped her at home after the party on Saturday and took a cab to his place. He'd wanted to spend the night, but he'd had an early meeting on Sunday morning that he needed to prepare for. They had a few brief phone conversations and some texts, but that was it. He'd arrived at work a few minutes early this morning to see her before his first conference call, but apparently Dana had opened today and Zoe wouldn't be in until later on. Wasn't that something he should know as her . . . whatever the hell he was?

He'd felt so good about where things were between them a few days ago, but now he wondered how he'd ever see her with the hectic lifestyle they both lived. Zoe had been right about one thing—they spent a lot of time at their respective jobs. Zoe was the owner of a growing business and she was very hands-on, which was crucial in those first years. Dylan completely understood and supported that. And his family was very much the same. Not a one of them was a goof-off playboy. They all worked their ass off handling their properties. He tried to make time to blow off steam whenever possible, but some of his weeks were just downright hellish and this was shaping up to be one of them. His brief spell of playing Angry Birds while he tried to figure out what Zoe was doing last week had landed him behind on some presentations. So in between numerous meetings with what seemed like everyone in Florida, and a constant load of telephone and video conferences, it promised to be even more hectic than usual.

When he reached his office, he took a moment to pull his cell phone out and shoot Zoe a quick text. Missed you at the shop. Dinner meeting tonight. I'll try to come down at some point to see that beautiful face. It hardly conveyed what he was feeling, but it was the best he had right now. They were on uncharted ground and each move was a learning experience. He wasn't comfortable with coming on too strong, too soon. So he thought a balance between their usual relationship with a bit more thrown in was a good place to start.

Hell, he shocked the shit out of himself Saturday night when he'd told her some of how he was feeling. He was still terrified that he was making a mistake, but there was no way he could stand around while the Joshes of the world took the woman who he'd become so possessive of out on dates and God only knew what else. And sadly, Josh was bad, but then he'd had an even scarier thought. She was bound to eventually meet a nice guy. One who had thoughts of her, a white picket fence, a minivan, and a couple of kids on his mind. Even he knew that she fit in that picture perfectly. Maybe that made him a selfish bastard because he had no clue if that was something he could ever offer her. Hell, he'd never even seriously entertained the thought of getting married, much less having kids. But dammit, he couldn't let her go without knowing where things could go between them if they gave it a shot.

One thing the other evening had taught him was that he needed to clean up his backyard pronto. He couldn't have a repeat of the Carey/Kristen episode. It wasn't as if he had women throwing themselves at him all the time. But he'd been known to kick back by having sex with some of the women who ran in his crowd. Not all were as outspoken as Carey and Kristen, but there were enough of them to give him a case of anxiety. He hated to say it, but possibly he needed to cultivate some new friends. He'd gone to college with most of the ones he hung out with now and some had never left the frat brother stage. The more settled ones tended to meet them for a beer once a month, but skipped the parties for obvious reasons.

He was still mulling it over when Lisa knocked on his door and stepped inside a few moments later. "Good morning, boss," she grumbled as she came forward and took a seat in front of him. He grinned as he almost always did at her snarky mood. He'd learned early on that Lisa wasn't a morning person, which suited him perfectly. She came in every morning for a brief hello and to see if he had anything urgent for her to take care of. They tended to leave each other alone after that until after lunch, when they'd run through the schedule for tomorrow and any other matters that needed to be addressed before the next day.

"Morning, sunshine." He smirked, thinking he must be insane to enjoy this so much. "How's my favorite assistant on this early Monday morning?"

"Peachy." She grimaced before taking a big drink from her coffee cup. He saw Zoe's logo on the side of it and grinned like the sap he was becoming. "So I guess we're actually working this week, huh? I kind of enjoyed your slacking for those few days. Plus, I noticed you got a high score on Angry Birds. I'll load Candy Crush for you today if you want to try something new."

He laughed, shaking his head at her. "I'd love to,

but I had to work half the night to make up for that so I guess it's business as usual for both of us."

"Well, that sucks," she sighed. "You might as well give me the list of what you want taken care of first and I'll attempt it after I've woken up." He handed her some notes for another presentation she was helping him with and she got to her feet. She was almost at the door before she turned, giving him such a smug grin that alarm bells were going off inside him. "So . . . you and Zoe, huh? I'd like to say it's a surprise, but not so much."

Staring at her in surprise, Dylan asked, "How did you know?" He wasn't sure why he was shocked. For such a big place, the employees of the Oceanix seemed to stay well informed on all the latest gossip. Hell, Lisa usually caught him up on anything he'd missed in that area at least a few times a week. He hadn't known that she was friends with Zoe, though. *Dana.* It had to have come from Zoe's friend and employee. That made perfect sense.

Shrugging, Lisa said, "Oh, you know, I just heard someone mention it. Anyway, that's not important. I think it's awesome. You two are perfect for each other." Wagging her finger, she added, "Try not to screw it up. She's not one of your . . . usual types, so it'll require a little more from you than dinner at McDonald's and thirty minutes at your place."

"Thirty minutes?" he choked out. "I think you've

got me confused with someone else. I'm thirty-four, not seventy."

She giggled, knowing she'd hit her mark in questioning his stamina. What man didn't get defensive about that? "No judgment," she called out as she left. He could still hear her laughter from the outer office. Maybe it was worth the insult if it put her in a good mood this early in the day. Then a thought occurred to him and he picked up his phone and buzzed her desk. "What? I just left."

"Calm down, this won't require anything major on your part. Could you please make sure that I leave around twelve for lunch?"

"Sure," she agreed. He heard her fingers clicking on her keyboard before she said, "I don't show anything scheduled, though. Who is the meeting with and I'll go ahead and key in it?"

"I—er . . . it's personal," he stumbled, feeling strangely embarrassed. Some men might have their secretaries send flowers and gifts to the woman in their life, but that had never been an issue for him.

There was dead silence for a few seconds before he heard the humor return to her voice. "Ohhh, I see. I'll just put Zoe's name in. And don't worry, you'll make it if I have to drag you out by your tie."

Dylan shook his head ruefully as he pulled up his e-mail and got started with his day. Apparently, having a significant other was something everyone in his life would have to adjust to. He had a feeling that his well-ordered existence was about to be turned up on its ear and he'd never been happier at that prospect.

❧

"Lover boy was here looking for you this morning." Dana smirked before making a kissy face. "He was so disappointed when I told him you wouldn't be in till later. He said he'd try to come back during lunch."

Feeling her mood lighten considerably, Zoe said, "Really? Did he say anything else?" *God, I sound like a teenager.*

"Nope, that was pretty much it." Dana smiled knowingly. "I will say that he was looking flipping fine in that suit. That man certainly knows how to pull off the *GQ* look. I mean, don't get me wrong, he's no Paul, but then again, who is?"

Zoe smiled as she wiped the counter down before refilling the blueberry muffins that had flown off the shelf that morning. "I take it things are still going well between you two?"

Wiggling her brows, Dana said, "They're amazing. We're getting along far better this time. I think we really needed some time apart to appreciate what we had together. He's really making an effort to spend more time with me. Last night we went out to dinner with Mike and had a great time."

"Wait." Zoe gaped at her friend. "You spent the evening with the man that you left Paul for, but then left to go back to Paul? And you had a great time?" When Dana nodded as if not understanding the big deal, Zoe rubbed her forehead in amazement. "You guys are really nuts, or you're the most understanding people I've ever met. I don't think I could do that. Heck, I basically had some kind of jealous tantrum when we had to sit with two of Dylan's ex-bimbos at the party Saturday night. I sure wouldn't want to go have a drink with them."

"What?" Dana screeched out, and then lowered her voice when Zoe shushed her. "You didn't mention that. I thought things were all lovey-dovey. It sounds as if you left out the best part."

Zoe motioned her to the corner so that they wouldn't be overheard before saying, "We were eating and these two Barbie dolls sat down at our table. They were hanging all over Dylan and asking to go back to his place for a repeat performance. They let it be known that they didn't mind doing him at the same time."

"Okay." Dana shrugged. "Don't let stuff like that bother you, honey. You know Dylan's given a ride or two. But he's never been in a relationship before, so you rank far above them. I hate it when women lower themselves to act like that, but unless he was encouraging them, you have to let it go. Just because you were a virgin the first time doesn't mean that he should be penalized for not being one."

"I hadn't thought of it like that," Zoe admitted. "And he was very uncomfortable with what they were doing. He kept trying to talk to me and ignore them. Finally, I couldn't take it anymore and I left. But he followed me quickly, so he couldn't have said much to them. It might not have bothered me as much had I known at that point where things stood between us. But we didn't have that talk until later. So I was depressed that he might meet up with them later after having slept with me the night before."

"I can understand that completely." Dana patted her shoulder sympathetically. "That's always the hardest part of being with someone new. You have to deal with the uncertainty of whether they like you as much as you do them. And with men it's even worse because most are so paranoid about commitment that you have to watch what you say or you'll scare them off. Unless there's some amazing sex involved to take your mind off the other stuff, it can just plain suck. Mmm, speaking of that, lookie what's coming your way, girl."

Zoe's head flew up and her eyes connected with Dylan's. *Oh God, he looks good. I want him to take me upstairs and do dirty things to me right now.* She grinned at him as he drew closer, then wondered, *Do we hug? Kiss? High-five?* Thankfully, Dylan saved her from further obsessing by walking right up and dropping a gentle kiss onto her surprised mouth. "Good-bye, Dana," he called out, then waved without looking away from Zoe. She heard her friend huff in mock annoyance before walking back to the counter. "Can you have lunch with me, beautiful?" he asked as he twirled a strand of her hair around his finger.

Even though she'd been at the shop for barely an hour, she agreed without thought. "I'd love to, handsome. Want me to fix us some sandwiches and we can eat in my office?"

"That's the best offer I've had all day." He smiled. "I'll get the drinks. Lemonade?" He knew she had a weakness for the tart drink so he was already shooing Dana out of the way and adding ice to two glasses. Zoe hurried into the kitchen and pulled out the ingredients for gourmet grilled cheese sandwiches. She'd made them so many times that it required no more than a few minutes before she was plating them along with potato salad and a pickle spear. Dylan was waiting for her when she stepped through the double doors and led the way to her private space. She set their plates on the desk and turned to close the door behind him. Dana gave her a thumbs-up, which had Zoe biting back a smile. She was retracing her steps when Dylan reached out and pulled her into his lap. She laid her arms loosely on his shoulders as he nuzzled her neck. "Mmm, you smell good."

"It's the coffee," she sighed as his tongue circled the shell of her ear.

"I've missed you, sweetheart," he surprised her by

admitting. "I'm sorry things have been so crazy since Saturday. I thought about coming over last night, but it was already midnight and I knew you'd be in bed."

"You have a key," she pointed out. "You could have let yourself in. I'd be happy just to have you near."

"Yeah?" he murmured as he kissed the corner of her lips before fitting his mouth firmly over hers. Their lunch was quickly forgotten as he moved her around until she was straddling his lap. She'd worn a short summer dress today, which left very little fabric between her damp core and his now hard cock. "I want you so fucking badly," he hissed as he pushed her hips down while raising his to meet hers. "Shit, we need to stop while I can."

When he slowed, Zoe grabbed his wrist, saying urgently, "I need you now. Don't stop." He looked at her in awe before setting her gently on her feet and getting to his own. He unzipped his pants and pushed them along with his boxer briefs down around his ankles. He ran a hand under her skirt and growled his pleasure when he found her wet and ready for him.

"Bend over the desk," he ordered, suddenly all alpha male.

Heat surged through her body as she scrambled to comply with his demand. Considering this was only the second time she'd had sex, she felt like she'd gone from training wheels to a Harley in the blink of an eye, and she absolutely loved it. The men in the books had nothing on the one currently palming her ass before flipping her dress up. "My panties," she whispered as she attempted to move away long enough to pull them off.

"They stay," he insisted. *Oookay.* Granted, she didn't have a lot of experience, but she was pretty sure the tiny piece of silk separating them needed to go in order to connect the boy and girl parts together. Maybe he was simply going to finger her again, and while that was exciting, it wasn't what she had in mind today. *But why would he have taken his pants off for that?* Well, she'd never gotten a hand job nor had a guy jack off in her office. He was definitely giving her some more firsts today. When he nudged her panties to the side and she felt the head of his cock pressing into her, she jerked in shock. *Yes!* She was pathetically eager to discover that they were indeed having sex and a little sheepish that she hadn't thought of the whole moving-the-underwear thing. "Ready?" he asked as he circled his hips against her.

"God yes," she moaned, sounding like some of the women she made fun of in porn movies. She had to think, though, that maybe they hadn't been acting after all. The fit was incredibly tight as Dylan pushed into her slowly. The pressure was so intense that she wanted to widen her stance, but he kept her legs firmly between his own, controlling her movements. "Ohhh, Dylan," she cried, then bit her lip, not wanting anyone in the shop to hear them.

He seated himself the last few inches, then paused for a moment to let her adjust. She moved her hips back against him impatiently and he chuckled before swatting her ass. "Patience, baby. I'll take care of you." Then without warning, he pulled almost completely out and plunged back in. "Fuck yeah," he groaned as he set a fast rhythm. His balls were slapping against her as he bottomed out on each hard thrust.

Zoe was so close that she was shaking with the need to come. She ground against him, trying to get the friction that she needed to push her over the edge. She gritted her teeth and whimpered as she continued to climb higher. Her body was as taut as a bow as she chased her release. "Dylan . . . I need," she gasped out, not knowing how to put what she was feeling into words. He seemed to know, though, as his hand reached around her and found her clit. With a few firm strokes to the sensitive bud, she was shattering around him.

"Shhh, baby," he reminded her as he continued to pump into her wet heat until she felt him stiffen and jerk inside her. He moved in and out in a more leisurely fashion now as they both rode out their peak until he dropped a kiss onto her shoulder and pulled out. He grabbed a tissue from the box on her desk and wrapped his condom up in it. She hadn't even seen him put it on and was grateful that he'd had the presence of mind to protect them, because she certainly hadn't thought of it. Maybe it was time to go on birth control so that they always had a backup in place. She was glad to have a small adjoining bathroom so that she could clean up quickly. She pulled the door closed behind her, not quite ready to share so much intimacy with Dylan even though they'd just had sex.

When she walked back into her office a few moments later, he had one plate arranged on the desk and both of their glasses. "Have you already eaten?" she asked, wondering if she'd been gone longer than she thought.

Giving her a rueful grin, he pointed to the trashcan. "One of our body parts ended up in it. I thought we could share this one." Zoe laughed, hardly able to believe that they'd rolled on her grilled cheese while having hot sex in her office. It was official, she was a wild woman. She took the chair beside him and reached up to smooth his hair down without thinking. He looked surprised by the gesture, but not unpleased. "Thanks, babe."

"You go ahead and eat the whole thing. I'll make something for myself after you're gone," she offered.

Waving the sandwich in front of her, he asked, "Are you sure? This looks amazing." She motioned for him to take it all and he devoured his meal as if he'd worked up quite an appetite. When he was finished, he stood and pulled her into his arms once again. "I wish I could stay longer, but I have a busy afternoon. I think I can get away at a decent time tonight, though, if you want to have dinner."

"I'd like that," Zoe said softly. "How about I cook something for us so you can relax?"

He tucked her hair behind her ear as his finger stroked her cheek. "You'll be on your feet all afternoon, sweetheart. Why don't we have dinner at the restaurant here? Maybe you can run home and pack a bag so you can spend the night. Then we'll both be close to work tomorrow."

Zoe hesitated as visions of Carey and Kristen sleeping in his bed flashed through her head. Then she remembered Dana's earlier advice and realized that she was going to have to let that go if she was going to be involved with Dylan. She couldn't judge him for having a sexual past just because she didn't. Giving him a big smile, she nodded, saying, "That sounds perfect. Call me later on when you know what time you'll be free." They shared one last kiss before Dylan pulled away and opened her office door. He took a few steps, then stopped so abruptly that she plowed right into his back. "What?" she asked in confusion.

"Well, there's my daughter and her . . . friend." Zoe cringed when she peaked around Dylan's shoulder and saw her mother standing there with a knowing grin on her face. Dana stood off to the side, shooting her an apologetic grimace.

"Hello again, Vivian." He turned sideways to Zoe, saying, "I had a meeting with your mother earlier to go over the restaurant budget and projections for the next quarter."

"That's um . . . nice," Zoe muttered as she met her mother's amused gaze.

"Dana told me that you two had gone out for lunch, but I was almost sure I heard . . . voices from this direction. Decided to eat in?" Oh, good Lord, what was her mother doing? Surely she hadn't meant that last question to sound as dirty as it came out. Of course, knowing her as Zoe did, she was probably enjoying watching her daughter squirm. A quick glance at Dylan showed that he was thinking the same thing. Instead of looking embarrassed, his lips twitched as if fighting back laughter. "So while I have you two together, I wanted to ask if you'd have dinner with Marcus and me tonight. It's not going to be anything fancy. I thought I'd grill some steaks and maybe twice-baked potatoes with green beans. How does that sound?"

"I . . . er—don't you have to work late tonight?" she asked Dylan, praying he would take the hint and play along.

But apparently, the man had no self-preservation skills because she looked at him incredulously as he said, "No, I told you I'd be off in time to have dinner. Since we were going to eat in the restaurant anyway, this actually works out well. Thanks for the invitation, Vivian. What time should we be there?" *Has he lost his mind? My mother knows we just had sex in my office and he's willing to go eat dinner with her now?*

Her mother actually clapped her hands, which was rather alarming to Zoe, before saying, "Perfect. Can you make it around seven? I know how busy you and Zoe get sometimes."

Was it her imagination or was there an extra emphasis on the word *busy*? She saw Dana biting her tongue and figured the other woman had noticed it too. Dylan continued to prove that he was completely oblivious when he said, "That should work well. I'm looking forward to it." He then turned to her and brushed a kiss across her startled lips before saying, "I've got to get back to work, sweetheart. I'll call you later." He smiled at her mother and Dana as he walked by. "Ladies. Have a good day." And with those parting words, the bastard was gone and she was left to deal with two of the nosiest people on earth.

Holding up her hand, she said, "I swear I don't want to hear a word. Dylan and I were just having lunch. There's no need to stand there looking like you caught me in the act."

Dana cleared her throat before handing her a napkin. "You might want to wipe the potato salad off your neck, sweetie. You were really a messy eater today."

Zoe felt her face flush with color as she wondered how she'd missed that when she was in the bathroom.

She had her answer as to what happened to the other plate now. Obviously, she'd lain in it at some point.

Her mother stepped forward and pulled something from the bottom of her dress. "You might need this sticky note. I believe it's about ordering supplies."

Closing her eyes in resignation, Zoe officially threw in the towel. Between the food on her chest and the sticky note stuck to her crotch area, there was no easy way to play this one off. If she was going to have sex in her office again, then Dylan would have to start looking her over before she went back out into public. "I give up." She tossed her hands in the air. "You caught me. Dylan and I rolled all over my desk. Happy now?"

Dana fell against the wall laughing while her mother gave her a satisfied smirk. "There, that wasn't so hard, was it, dear? It seems like when I'm not in the shop for a day, I miss a heck of a lot. When did you and Dylan go from being buddies to being butties?"

As Dana cackled at her mother's crude attempt at humor, Zoe shook her head and rolled her eyes. "Really? I'm your daughter. I'm not even supposed to be discussing stuff like this with you, much less having to deal with your off-color humor. I swear you better not say stuff like that around Dylan tonight."

Dana tossed her arm around Zoe's shoulders. "Sweetie, this is your first time with a walk of shame. Don't fight it. Just go with it. Trust me, it gets easier after a while.

Well . . . I'm not sure, though. since generally you hide that stuff from your parents."

"I'm trying!" Zoe snapped. Turning back to her mother, she added, "Dylan and I have decided to date and see where it takes us. We like each other as more than friends, but that's as far as we've gotten. So don't go knitting baby booties and Photoshopping him into our family pictures. No matter how things turn out, we're committed to remaining friends, so I'd appreciate it if you wouldn't scare the hell out of him and send him running."

"Oh, pooh," her mother said, and laughed. "That boy isn't the least bit intimidated by me. He would have pulled his zipper up in front of me without batting an eye."

"Oh, brother," Zoe moaned. "I need to get back to work. I'm sure we can discuss this later—or God willing, not."

As if conceding that she'd embarrassed her enough, her mother gave her a hug before saying, "I need to run along anyway. I'll see you tonight. Oh, and you might want to fix that hair a bit; you look like you were caught in a stiff wind." With that parting shot, she was gone and Dana was once again clutching her side at her mother's word choice.

"I absolutely love that woman," her friend giggled when she could catch her breath. "My parents are so uptight, but your mother is awesome. You're so freaking lucky."

Zoe felt some of her tension from being busted by her mommy fall away as she conceded that the other woman was right. She was damned lucky to have the mother who was always cool. When her friends had complained about their parents, she'd shrugged it off because she never had those issues. It wasn't that she was allowed to run wild or get away with everything. It was more that her mother allowed her the room to be a kid without tons of rules. Somehow that freedom was what kept her from going through the usual teenage hell years. She never had anything to rebel against so acting out seemed rather pointless. "She is pretty amazing," Zoe agreed. "She's not above humiliating me when the opportunity arises—shit, forget I said that." Could none of them speak without using some code word for sex or a dick?

As they walked back toward the counter, Dana grabbed her arm, bringing her to a halt. "Just so you know, you and Dylan need to bring the sex moans down about two levels the next time you get nasty. I couldn't hear you in the main shop, but you better be glad that Gladys in the kitchen is deaf as a doornail. Otherwise, she'd have been going home with quite a story to tell tonight."

"Good Lord," Zoe groaned before dropping her head. While her first public sex outing had been hot, it had also been somewhat of a disaster in the secret department. She wouldn't be surprised if the hotel concierge winked at her when she left this afternoon. From now on, when they did something like that, Dylan would simply have to gag her. But as crazy as things had been since they'd opened the office door, she couldn't regret it. She was actually living now instead of standing on the sidelines while everyone around her did. If that meant she had to suffer a little embarrassment every now and again, then it was a small price to pay to have Dylan and all that he had to offer in her life.

Eleven

With one hand on the wheel and the other on Zoe's knee, Dylan drove them through Pensacola to her mother's house. He'd managed to leave the office with just enough time to spare for a quick change of clothes before picking Zoe up. She'd obviously done the same because she was wearing a different dress than she'd had on earlier. It was probably a good thing because he didn't think he'd ever be able to see the other one again without getting instantly hard. *Don't think about sex this close to her mother's house. Vivian might chop your dick off.*

"I tried to get us out of this earlier, you know," she grumbled. "If you had just taken my hint, we'd be having a nice, quiet dinner in the restaurant with no one making snide comments about what we were doing in my office."

Dylan chuckled as he squeezed her fingers. "I'm sorry, babe. I thought we'd look guiltier if we didn't go. Plus, I like Vivian. She's a lot of fun and I know you enjoy spending time with her when you can. I didn't want you to miss out on that just because we got a little carried away over our lunch hour."

"That's actually very sweet," she said, and smiled. "I'm used to her after all these years. I just thought it might be a bit awkward for you because you know she's not likely to show you any mercy tonight, right? If you were harboring any hope that she'd gotten it all out of her system earlier, then I hate to burst your bubble, but she wouldn't let an opportunity like this go to waste. Plus, she'll probably have a glass of wine, which will loosen her up even more."

Strangely enough, he wasn't bothered by the thought. He had been around her mother enough at work to know her fairly well by now. And due to the fact that she'd worked at the Oceanix since he was a kid and he and her daughter were best friends as well meant that he'd always had a close relationship with her. In some ways, she was more like a mother to him than his own standoffish mother had ever been. Hell, he hadn't even seen his mother in two years now, but Vivian he saw almost daily. "It's not going to bother me," he assured her. "We're both adults, and if she wants to tease us about having sex, then more power to her. She's probably been holding it inside for years waiting for it to happen."

Zoe laughed. "She's not the only one. Sometimes I thought I was destined to be the oldest living virgin alive. It never bothered me that much until thirty became such a close reality. Somehow that just seemed—old."

Now that she'd brought it up, he jumped to ask her about it since he'd been damned curious. "Why did you wait so long? I mean, I know you've been busy getting the shop up and going for the last few years, but what about before that? Never anyone that tempted you?"

She shifted in her seat before putting her hand over his on her knee. "I guess not," she said lightly. "And as I got older, it seemed a shame to let my first time be with just anyone. So I ended up being twenty-nine and you know the rest of the story."

Dylan thought there was a lot she wasn't saying, but he understood that it was a very personal thing and he didn't want to make her uncomfortable. Besides, if she hadn't have waited, then he wouldn't have been her only lover, and that was something that he liked more than he could have ever imagined. It made him feel crazy possessive of her knowing that he was the only man to ever have her in that way. The fact that he'd taken her bent over her desk at lunch in the coffee shop was a prime example of how nuts she made him. Even with Vivian and Dana laughing their asses off afterward, he would have still done it again in a heartbeat. Hell, he'd been at war with himself all afternoon to keep from begging her to come up to his office and try out the desk there. Lisa would no doubt love heckling him over that. "I can't say that I'm sorry about that, sweetheart," Dylan admitted as he turned into Vivian's driveway.

Zoe's mother lived in a small house on the bay side of Santa Rosa Island. This area had been largely untouched by commercial development, and he enjoyed the peaceful feel as he walked around and helped Zoe from the car. "Are you ready for this?" she joked as her mother stood in the door motioning them forward.

"Is it my imagination, or is she way too cheerful? I've known your mother forever and I've seen her smile more today than in all the other years combined. Shit, I didn't even know she had that many teeth," Dylan joked while watching the older woman warily. He'd wondered how she'd feel about Zoe being intimately involved with him, and so far, she appeared to be pleased. Either that or she was setting him up first, then planning to knock his balls down his throat later on.

"Yeah, I can't remember the last time she was actually waiting for me when I arrived," Zoe said out of the corner of her mouth. "It's not too late to fake a work emergency or a stomach problem."

Escape didn't sound like a bad idea, but Vivian would call him on it in a minute. He didn't think now was the time to look like a spineless wimp. Plus, he had visions of her insisting on coming to the bathroom with him to confirm his story, so that was definitely out. How bad could a few hours be? They'd have dinner, make a little small talk, then be on their way. As long as the night ended with Zoe in his bed, he could survive anything.

"Darlings, right on time." Vivian pulled each of them into a hug before waving them through the door ahead of her. "Marcus is just finishing up at the grill so let's go on through to the kitchen. Zoe, why don't you fix us both a glass of wine while I'm setting the table."

"Sure, Mom." As Zoe crossed to a cabinet and stretched to get some glasses down, Dylan found his eyes glued to her ass. Shit, he could feel himself getting hard as once again he remembered how amazing it felt to be inside her today. She was so unbelievably tight and—

When he felt a hand on his shoulder, he almost jumped out of his skin. "Feeling okay, Dylan? You're a bit flushed. Must be hotter in here than I thought." Shit, Vivian. *You are so busted.*

"I . . . um . . . no. I'm fine. It's the humidity," he fumbled, feeling like a teenage boy caught jacking off. Vivian's amused expression said that she knew exactly, or pretty damn close, what he'd been thinking. God, he hoped she was off at least a bit on that. He had to get it together and stop ogling her daughter while she was in the vicinity. The woman was enjoying his discomfort far too much.

Luckily, Vivian's boyfriend, Marcus, stepped through the patio doors with their steaks and Vivian was distracted. Marcus set the plate on the counter then stepped forward with his hand extended. "Good to see you again, Dylan." Then the other man looked over at Vivian before adding, "Feeling brave tonight, huh?" Dylan swallowed audibly, thinking maybe he had made a mistake in coming before the other man said, "Don't let her get to you. She's actually thrilled that things have progressed between you and her daughter. She just enjoys giving you a hard time."

Relaxing slightly, Dylan nodded. "Thanks for the heads-up. I was considering raising the white flag, then running like hell."

"What are you two whispering about?" Zoe grinned knowingly as she handed Dylan a glass of wine that was so full, he had a hard time raising it to his mouth without spilling some. Obviously her plan to survive was alcohol. Wine didn't do much to take his edge off, but he thought it might look bad to ask for hard liquor when he'd be the one driving them home.

"Marcus was telling me that he hid all the knives and locked the guns away."

Zoe giggled before shooting a glance at her mother, who was humming under her breath as she put the finishing touches on their meal. "She looks so innocent, doesn't she? In her defense, she's been waiting a long time to torture one of my dates, so try to go with it."

Smiling at the woman, who above all else was still his best friend, Dylan dropped a kiss on her forehead before saying, "Anything for you, sweetheart. I'll always have your back." And that, he thought, was the absolute truth. There might be uncertainty in the rest of their relationship but he couldn't imagine a day when he wouldn't give everything he had to see that beautiful smile on her face that she seemed to reserve only for him. *God, never let me lose that.*

～

As the whole meet-the-parent things went, Zoe had to admit that it wasn't just a horrible evening. Her mother had taken most of her best shots at the coffee shop earlier, so it was mostly a relaxed affair. Of course, the two heaping glasses of wine that she drank might have had something to do with that. Dylan and Marcus got along well and there was never a lapse in conversation. At one point Zoe had been horrified when her mother, looking deadly serious, pointed to Dylan and said, "If you knock her up, you marry her."

Dylan had knocked his glass of water over and they'd all scurried to clean it up before it drenched the entire table. He'd also got in a couple of good zings of his own. The first was asking Marcus what his intentions were toward her mother and also recommending a seniors' class that he'd read about that dealt with erectile dysfunction. Her mother had literally fallen on the floor laughing on that one, before assuring them that Marcus didn't have problems in that area. Luckily, Marcus was also a good sport and had no issues with being pulled into their crude humor.

"I actually had a good time tonight," Dylan admitted as they walked into his home on the top floor of the Oceanix. "I'll go ahead and admit that I wasn't expecting the case of condoms she handed to me on the way out the door, though. Can you believe she actually went in Costco and bought those? Hell, I don't know how I'm going to get them out of the car with the name 'Trojan' written all over the box."

"Please do it when I'm not with you." Zoe laughed. "I was happy to see that they were the 'ribbed for her pleasure' variety. That was very thoughtful of her, right?"

Pulling her into his arms, Dylan palmed her ass, giving it a firm squeeze. "Doesn't it freak you out that she has given so much thought to our sex life? I swear I wouldn't have been shocked if she'd given me a gallon of lube to go with them."

"Well, she did tell you not to use petroleum jelly with the latex," Zoe pointed out. Okay, maybe the evening had been a little worse than she'd initially remembered. But by that time, everything had seemed more amusing than anything else. Especially Dylan's nonreaction to it. You'd have thought he was discussing the weather with her mother rather than wrapping it up.

"Yeah, let's not forget that." Dylan shuddered. "If I can't perform tonight, then you'll know she got in my head."

Feeling bold, Zoe lowered her hand to cup his already impressive bulge. "I don't see a problem here so far."

Dylan had his hand up her shirt, flicking her nipple through the thin material of her bra, when his phone sounded from nearby. "Fuck," he hissed. He looked torn, but finally pulled away. "I have to check the damn thing in case it's the hotel." He picked up his cell phone from the coffee table and winced. "It's just Josh. I'll call him back later." He was in the process of putting the phone down when it chimed with a text. He scowled when he clicked a few buttons, Zoe assumed to read it. "Dammit! Josh is at a bar drunk and needing a ride home." Running a hand through his hair, he said, "I don't want to go, but if I don't and something happens—"

"Dylan, you have to go," Zoe interrupted him. "I'll be right here when you get back. Just take care of your friend and make sure he gets home in one piece." He gave her a lingering kiss good-bye and promised to be back in an hour, tops. She waved him away, knowing he felt bad about leaving.

After he was gone, she kicked off her shoes and settled onto his plush leather sofa. She grinned at his collection of remote controls on the coffee table. Thank-

fully she'd been here enough to know which one operated the television. She flipped channels for a while
before running across the Lifetime Network and what
looked like a good suspense movie. Within moments
she was engrossed, and when it ended two hours
later, she looked around in surprise. Dylan still wasn't
home. She didn't want to distract him from driving by
calling or texting, but she was getting worried.

When another hour came and went, she picked up
her phone and sent him a quick text asking if everything
was okay. Then she waited . . . and waited, but he didn't
respond. By this time, she was pacing the floor. *They've
been in an accident. Maybe I should try the hospital. No, I
should call him first.* Quickly hitting the speed dial for his
number, she almost dropped the phone when she heard
loud noise in the background, along with laughter and
then a voice that was unmistakably Dylan's said, "Yeah?"
Yeah? That's all I rate after he disappears for three hours?

"Um . . . Dylan?" she asked, just to make sure it was
indeed him, even though she was certain it was.

"You've got him, sweetheart." Zoe pulled the phone
away for a moment, staring at it as if it had bitten her
before putting it back to her ear. It wasn't as if she had
a problem with what he'd said; it was the fact that he
sounded completely wasted.

"I was getting worried. You were supposed to be back
a few hours ago. I—wanted to make sure that everything
was okay."

"Sorry, babe," he said, not sounding sincere in the least. "It's Josh's birthday and they're having a party for him tonight. Must have slipped my mind earlier. But it's all good."

"Sounds like the ball and chain is giving my buddy hell," she heard someone who sounded like Josh say in the background. "Why don't you ask Mom for permission to stay out a little later, man. Get them balls back from her while you're at it."

Then instead of telling his friend off, Dylan laughed before making a halfhearted attempt at quieting his friend. "Go away, bro. I'll be over there in a second. Sorry 'bout that—you know how he is."

"Sure," Zoe said flatly. It wasn't that she was angry about him being out with the guys. It was the fact that he'd left her here and basically disappeared while she'd been expecting him back soon. Was it too much to ask that he let her know he'd decided to stay?

"I shouldn't be much longer. I'm just going to hang out for a little longer then I'll catch a cab home. Miss you."

Is he kidding me right now? He misses me? Instead of saying any of the dozens of retorts on the tip of her tongue, she settled for, "Be careful."

She heard Josh or someone that sounded like him urging Dylan to get off the phone and have another drink. "Listen, I'll see you soon, babe."

Not here you won't, she thought to herself. "Sure, good night." With that, she ended the call and immediately begin putting her shoes back on. The evening was ruined for her, and there was no way she was going to stay here any longer waiting for him to decide to come home. He was probably too busy with Carey, Kristen, and whatever other bimbos were hanging around their group tonight.

She knew that Dylan had a life and friends outside of her, which had never bothered her before. But now she had to wonder why he'd kept her separated from the rest of his buddies. They'd been friends for years; shouldn't she have spent more time with his other friends as well? Sure, he wouldn't want her along if they were going out with the sole intention of picking up women, but there had to be times, such as the cookout, when it was just a group getting together. Had he been embarrassed about their relationship? She might not have been the best dresser through the years, but she hadn't been that bad, had she?

Now she had to wonder exactly what went on when all the guys got together. If it was bad enough that he had never wanted her around them, then what where they doing tonight? Drinking certainly; that much had been apparent. This was a side of Dylan that the friendship Zoe could deal with easier than the undefined relationship Zoe. She didn't like feeling as if she was an afterthought to him. She picked up his hotel extension and dialed the concierge to ask him to order her a taxi. She might be new to this whole being-involved situation, but she'd learned one thing from her mother long ago. You never waited around for a man to make you a priority. To do that set a precedent for something Zoe wasn't willing to do, even for Dylan.

Twelve

Dylan winced as a shrill sound filled the air. When it became obvious that it wasn't going to stop, he rolled over onto his back and looked for the source. His alarm clock was raising holy hell, and it took at least another two minutes until he was coordinated enough to switch it off. Shit, it was already six in the morning. Most of the time he awoke well before his alarm, but he'd only been in the bed a few hours, and God help him, it was Tuesday morning so there was no possibility of sleeping late.

Muttering a string of obscenities, he rubbed his blurry eyes and attempted to pry his tongue from the roof of his dry mouth. His body was sluggish so it took more precious time before he was able to move into a sitting position. Hell, he knew better than to do any major drinking on a work night. Not that every day wasn't that for him, but the weekends had a bit more leeway than the others. Still, when Josh had called and asked for a ride, he'd felt honor bound to go get him. Then he'd discovered that most of their friends were at the bar celebrating Josh's birthday, something he'd completely forgotten about. As soon as he'd stepped into the bar, a drink had been thrust into his hand— then another and so forth. He'd been unusually careless and hadn't bothered to keep track of how much he was putting away as he stood around socializing with some of their old friends that he hadn't seen in a while.

Oh fuck. Then it hit him like a ton of bricks. Where was Zoe? He'd left her here promising to be back in an hour and it had been more like five hours at least. He felt like an absolute bastard because he'd been so wasted when he got home that he hadn't even missed her. Wait—hadn't she called last night? Everything was fuzzy, but he was almost certain he remembered talking to her. Grabbing his phone, he flipped through the call log and indeed saw a three-minute call from her cell phone. Then he checked his texts and found one from her as well. *This isn't good*, he thought as he stumbled to his feet and made a quick pass through the apartment, thinking she could have possibly slept on the sofa. But there was no sign of her. Obviously she'd decided to go home . . . quite possibly pissed off at him. *It hasn't even been a week and you've fucked up. You're rocking this relationship thing.* How had she gotten home? He'd picked her up for dinner at her mother's last night so she didn't have her car. He figured she'd called a cab, but he'd worry until he knew for sure that she'd made it home safely. *Little late to be wondering that now, isn't it?*

He quickly pulled up the contact in his phone for the coffee shop and tried it. If she was opening today, she should be there by now. But when the phone was answered, he recognized Dana's voice right away. *Just what I need this morning.* He debated hanging up, but figured she would probably *69 his ass and call right back. "Hey, is Zoe in yet?"

"May I ask who's calling, please?" He stifled his irritation even though he knew damn well that she was aware it was him. Even this early, she liked jerking his chain.

"It's Dylan. Is your *boss* in yet?" If he thought he'd get to her by reminding her that she was an employee, it didn't hit the mark.

"Nope, she's not." And that was it. They both remained on the line while she waited for him to beg for the information that he wanted. God, how could Zoe stand her?

"Do you mind telling me when she will be?" he asked in a voice full of sarcasm.

"Shouldn't you already know that?" she asked sweetly. "You two are dating after all. So if Zoe didn't tell you her schedule, then maybe I'm not supposed to either. I don't want my *boss* to be angry with me. How about I just leave her a message to call you when she does get in? Or better yet, if you have her cell number, you could give that as try. She usually prefers a text, so I'd go with that. Especially if there's a reason that she might be avoiding your call." *I swear this woman hates me. What a bitch.*

Refusing to let her see that she'd struck a chord, he said, "You've been very helpful. Thanks so much. I'll be sure to pass my appreciation along to your *boss* when I speak with her. Now have a good day."

He was in the process of disconnecting the call, feeling a childish urge to have the last word, when he heard her call out, "Why, thank you, Mr. Jackson, you too." Then a click sounded in his ear and he knew he'd been bested yet again. *Another round to Dana. She owns you.*

His throat was dry and scratchy so he walked into the kitchen and got a bottle of water from the refrigerator. Without closing the door, he turned it up and drained most of it before setting it aside and trying Zoe's cell. And as luck would have it, the call went straight to voice mail. Next he pulled up his text screen with his fingers hovering over the keys for five solid minutes as he tried to decide what to write. Finally, he settled for, Wanted to make sure you made it home okay. Please call or text me back. I'm sorry about last night. I can explain. Xoxo.

Had he seriously just typed the symbol for hugs and kisses for the very first time to Zoe? Hell, he'd never sent that to a woman before. If not for seeing it all over Facebook and the Internet, he wouldn't have even known what it stood for. Wait—maybe he'd better check to make sure he was right. Oh crap, maybe it meant, "I love you." He wasn't sure now. He did a Google search and sagged in relief. No, he was right the first time. It wasn't that he didn't love Zoe, because he did. She was his best friend after all. But with them in some sort of relationship now, it might seem weird to say that. Especially after his fuck-up from the previous night.

Dylan took a quick shower, leaving his phone sitting on the bathroom counter in case she called. Then he dried his hair with his phone propped against the mirror so he could see the screen, since he couldn't hear it. He carried the damn thing in his hand constantly until he left at eight to go down to the office. He wanted to drop by the shop, but didn't think he could keep himself from killing Dana if Zoe weren't there to intercede. Of course, after last night, she might hand the other woman a knife and let her go at him. Hell, he even kinda deserved it.

When Lisa walked in a few moments later with her

usual cup of coffee, he pounced on her. "Was Zoe there? Did you see her?"

Giving him a pitying look, Lisa shook her head. "Nope. It was Dana and the other girl that usually works mornings. I don't remember her name, though." Putting her hands on her hips, she asked, "You're already in the doghouse, aren't you? Geez, Dylan, I thought you'd at least make it a few weeks before you messed up." Parking herself in her usual morning seat, she leaned forward, looking way too excited. "So . . . what'd you do?" First Dana and now Lisa. His assistant normally couldn't string three words together before ten in the morning, but today she was wide awake. *Lucky me.*

Shrugging, he strove for a casual I'm-not-a-bastard tone before admitting, "I had to pick up Josh from a bar last night. Then I ended up staying a little longer than expected because it was his birthday."

She looked vaguely disappointed as she asked, "So you had to break your plans with Zoe? That's nothing major, I'm sure she understood."

And this is where she names me asshole of the month. Wait for it. "Well, not exactly." He saw her eyes sharpen and her nose twitch as if she scented something good just around the corner. "Zoe and I were together when he called. Actually we were at my place. I told her I'd be back in an hour at about ten or so. But one thing led to another and it was a little later than I'd originally planned when I got home."

"How much later?" she asked with wide eyes. *Shit.*

"Around three," he choked out. *It sounds so much worse saying it aloud.*

"Dylan, good grief. You ditched your date for five hours to hang out with the boys? No wonder you two had a big fight when you got home. I'd have been seriously angry over that."

And go ahead and add the final nail in your coffin. "Um . . . we didn't argue. Actually, I took a cab home and passed out. I didn't remember until this morning that she should have been there. Obviously she left at some point and went home. So I've been trying to reach her this morning to make sure she got home all right."

"*Dylan,*" she gasped out. "What an asshole thing to do to anyone, but especially Zoe. Why in the world would you let that happen? I mean, I know most of your friends are selfish pricks, but you're usually better than that. And we're talking about Zoe here. Even if you guys weren't seeing each other now, she's still your best friend. You've always been careful of her feelings so what in the hell happened?"

"I don't know," he admitted as he slumped back in his chair. This was worse than he'd initially thought if Lisa was that horrified. "I guess I'm not used to worrying

201

about stuff like that when I'm out. I know that's no excuse, but it's all I've got right now."

She studied him for a moment before saying, "I think that possibly you were staging a little rebellion against being in a relationship. No matter how many excuses you make, that type of behavior isn't you. Don't get me wrong, I know you blow off steam with the guys, which is normal. But to leave a woman at your home, get loaded, and basically forget she was even there? That's a whole new level of douchery there."

"That makes no sense," he protested. "Why would I do something like that? I simply lost count of the number of drinks I had. I'd never do anything to intentionally hurt Zoe of all people. You know how I feel about her."

Getting to her feet, Lisa said softly, "Yeah I do, but I'm wondering if you do. Maybe you should look into that, boss. Now, if you're finished dumping all your personal problems on me, I need to go meditate at my desk for a few hours. This whole thing has exhausted me. You're not paying me enough for this level of emotional involvement. If you and Zoe stay together, I'm going to need a raise soon because I envision a lot more of these chats before you finally get it together." And with that parting shot, she walked out, slamming the door far too loudly behind her. *Does every woman in my life have PMS today?*

⌒

"You have got to be shitting me," Dana hissed as Zoe gave her a summary of what had occurred the previous night. "He left you home and went out with the guys?"

"Well, not exactly. I mean, he said he was picking up Josh because he'd had too much to drink. He was supposed to be home in an hour, but when I called him three hours later, he was drunk or darn close to it. And it was like he was brushing me off. Heck, I'm not even sure he knew who he was talking to. Then he called me at six this morning. Can you believe that? So now I have to wonder, was that what time he got home? If so, where did he spend the night? I don't think bars are open that long."

"I'm glad I gave him hell this morning," Dana snorted. "I wish I'd done worse. I knew something was up when he was trying to find you that early. Good for you not answering his call. He deserves to sweat this one out."

Zoe took a sip of her latte before staring glumly down at her desk. "I don't get it. Things went so well at dinner. Other than the condoms and some snide remarks, but that's my mother and he knows how she is. He was affectionate, attentive, and we just meshed so well together. When we got home, we were close to . . . you know, going to the bedroom, when damn Josh called. And truthfully, I wasn't angry. I'd have been disappointed in him if he had left a friend stranded. I relaxed and watched a movie, no big deal. Until I realized that two hours had passed, then another hour after I texted him. By that point I was worried that they'd been in an accident. I was completely blown away when he answered the phone and sounded three sheets to the wind. That was such an asshole thing to do to me and I didn't know how to handle it. That's not the Dylan I've always known. He calls me when we're going to hang out if he's running even a little late. So I still can't wrap my head around his behavior last night."

"He's a man, honey," Dana said as if that explained it all. "Sometimes their thought process is whacked. Plus, as much as I hate to defend him, you need to make allowances for a learning curve. Yes, absolutely he was a dick last night and he needs to grovel for your forgiveness. But this whole relationship thing is new for you both, and even though you'd hope an intelligent man like Dylan would know better than to commit such a rookie mistake, I guess he didn't. But if I know him, this will be one he won't forget. The fact that he was looking for you so early and sounding pretty damned concerned that you weren't here tells me that he knows he messed up, which is a good sign."

"I guess," Zoe said doubtfully. She still had a hard time reconciling his behavior with the man who had always been her friend. But maybe Dana had a point.

Also, since she didn't really have much of a social life, there wasn't that much that was changing in her world. Dylan, on the other hand, had a group that he'd been friends with since college and they all did get together on a regular basis. She'd wait and see what he had to say when he came down to see her. Because unless she missed her guess, he'd show up at some point today. He'd have to, because she didn't intend to return his call or text. He hadn't made it easy for her last night and she had no intention of making it easy for him today.

She was grateful that the usual morning rush hour left little time to dwell on the man who was just an elevator ride away. *I will not go to him.* She was cleaning tables during a lull when she felt someone touch her shoulder. She whirled around expecting either Dana or Dylan and was shocked to see Josh standing there instead. "Er . . . hi," she stuttered out. Josh had only ever been in her shop with Dylan, so his being here alone was quite unexpected. Maybe he was meeting Dylan.

"Good morning, Zoe." He smiled before putting his hands in his front pockets and rocking back on his heels.

When he didn't say anything else, she prompted, "Are you meeting someone? I can get you a coffee while you wait if you like."

"Actually I'm here to see you," he admitted. *Holy shit—why?*

Trying not to let him see that she was rattled, she

motioned to the table she'd just finished wiping down. "Want to have a seat? I only have a few minutes before I'll need to get back to work." *No way am I sitting here without an escape plan in place.* Dana shot her a "what the hell?" look from the counter, to which she shook her head, having no clue either.

He looked down at his hands before giving her a sheepish grin. "Listen, I talked to Dylan a little while ago and he told me about what happened last night. I know you two have been friends for longer than I've even known him and I can't help but feel that it's all my fault."

"You forced him to get drunk and forget that I was waiting for him?" she asked wryly. She wouldn't have pegged Josh as the type to care if his friend was in the hot seat with his kinda girlfriend. Actually, she figured he'd be more likely to be thrilled if Dylan was completely free of entanglements again.

"Kind of, yes. I did call him to take me home, knowing all along I wasn't ready to leave. I guess I was kind of bummed that he'd forgotten it was my thirtieth birthday and we always get together for things like that. It's sort of a standing thing with our old fraternity brothers. This is the first time that he'd missed something like that since college."

"I see," Zoe said thoughtfully, and she was beginning to get the picture. Josh, for all his seeming confidence and easygoing nature, had gotten his feelings hurt because one of his best friends had missed an important moment in his life. It still didn't excuse Dylan's behavior, but she was grateful that Josh had taken the time and effort to come offer an explanation.

"From the moment he walked in the door last night, either me or one of the others was shoving drinks in his hand. That's also the norm for those celebrations. You see, some of the guys are married now and have families so birthdays or special events are the only time they'll do more than drink a few beers before they go home. But everyone was drinking and having a good time last night so when Dylan showed up, he didn't stand much of a chance."

"And those comments you were making about me when I was on the phone with Dylan? Is that also part of the festivities for anyone who takes a call from a wife or girlfriend?"

Chuckling, he said, "Not really. That's called being so drunk you lose the filter that you normally have. I'm sorry about that. I don't really remember much of it, but I apologize for giving you a hard time. I hope you don't hold it against me. Dylan is one of my best friends and I know he's yours as well. In addition to whatever you guys are doing now."

"We're just seeing where this goes between us," Zoe admitted. "It's only been a few days, but it was going great until last night. I want to thank you, though, for coming to talk to me. Dylan's lucky to have you as a friend."

"I don't think he's feeling that way right now." Josh grimaced. "Maybe you could put in a good word for me when you forgive him."

Zoe noticed there was a line forming at the counter, so she pointed in that direction and got to her feet. "I've got to get back to work. But I appreciate this, Josh."

Josh stood as well and grinned when she extended a hand to him. "I think we can move past that now." He shocked her by pulling her in for a hug that lasted a few seconds longer than she was comfortable with.

"Er . . . okay," she muttered when she managed to break free. "See you later," she added before making her escape.

When he called after her, "You can count on it," she picked up her pace.

"I feel like wiping you down in hand sanitizer now," Dana whispered under her breath as she made a cappuccino for a customer. "Seriously, that guy gives me a creepy vibe."

Zoe rolled her eyes and attempted to shrug it off. A part of her agreed, though. Josh had always made her feel uncomfortable. He'd never really said or done anything out of line, but it was the way he looked at her. As if he could see beneath her clothes. Even before her mini-makeover, he'd had that effect on her. She'd always put it down to his personality and her limited experience with men in general. It made her grateful for Dylan. He may have been an asshole the evening before, but after a little groveling, she'd be forgiving him. She certainly didn't want to look at a future where there was nothing but one Josh after another. Whether he'd intended it or not, he'd helped his friend out of trouble more than he could have imagined.

Thirteen

I t wasn't one of his proudest moments, but when the front desk clerk called to tell him that Zoe had just entered the hotel, Dylan got to his feet hurriedly. He'd pondered just going down to the shop and working on his laptop until she arrived, but that would have meant way too much time with Dana. He wasn't sure Zoe would forgive him if he taped the other woman's mouth shut and locked her in the storage closet. So he'd asked John to let him know when she arrived. It was either that or watch the security feed for her car. Both pathetic, but that was the type of shit you were reduced to when you'd fucked up and the woman in question wasn't returning your calls or texts.

He was inches away from the door when it opened

and he found himself staring at his brother Asher. "What the hell are you doing here?" he asked in surprise. Ash ran the Charleston, South Carolina, location, so it wasn't as if he was in the neighborhood without a reason. He was closer to him than his other siblings, but today wasn't one he would have picked for an unannounced visit.

"Well, good to see you too," Ash said, grinning. "Lisa told me you had a stick up your ass today and I can see she's right as always."

"Just got a lot going on as usual. You should have told me you were coming."

"Now, where's the fun in that?" Ash smirked. "As it happens, I was visiting Charlotte, at her request of course, in Miami. She's staying at the hotel there for a few weeks."

Dylan leaned back against his desk, crossing his ankles. "You mean our *mother*?"

Ash took a seat in front of him before saying, "You know she prefers that we don't call her that, and let's face it, she's never exactly lived up to the title. Our pain-in-the-ass would be more accurate."

"Why in the world would you go all the way to Miami to see her? She certainly hasn't mentioned anything to me about being in Florida." Of course, considering his mother usually e-mailed him maybe once a month at best, it wasn't as if he stayed up-to-date on her activities.

Ash raised a brow as if to say, *Really, you need to ask?*

"The same old song and dance, brother. She wanted money and I guess it was my turn again. I swear I think she keeps a chart of all our names and marks them off as she goes down it. Then she starts over. Anything for that fucking worthless husband of hers. He's starting yet another business and needs some capital to get off the ground."

"Shit," Dylan muttered. "What's this one about? It's barely been a year since he was raving about being the next big gourmet food delivery service. I knew that was crap because it would have involved far too much work and execution for him."

"I think we should just buy him a fucking Taco Bell and call it a day," Ash deadpanned. "Those places never close and he could do what he does best, sit on his ass while someone else does the work."

Dylan had to admit, his brother's sarcastic idea did actually have some merit. In fact, it was downright brilliant. "You've got to suggest that. Hell, don't bother, just buy one and give them the deed. Then those two worthless kids of his can eat for free. If you could pull that off, we'd save enough money to open another Oceanix by year's end."

"You do know that was a joke, right?" Ash laughed as he nudged him out of the way and propped his feet on Dylan's mahogany desk. "Charlotte Jackson Dewalt would never lower herself to walk into a restaurant chain, much less own one."

Shaking his head in disgust, Dylan added, "She doesn't have a problem with asking her sons for money, though, does she? I swear, at some point we're going to have to cut her off. She already gets an allowance from Dad's estate, which is more than the average person could blow through in a year. But that goes through her fingers like water. Plus, she stays for free at any of our resorts, so it's not as if vacationing is breaking the bank for her."

"Trust me, I know," Ash agreed. "The only reason I bothered to go in person this time was because I felt like giving the asshole a hard time. But the joke was on me because I'm almost certain that our stepsister Claudia was hitting on me."

Dylan's mouth dropped open as he stared at his brother. "Man, please say you're kidding."

"Not even a bit." Ash winced. "If anything, I'm downplaying it."

"She's always been friendly," Dylan added. "Maybe you just took it the wrong way."

"And how exactly do you explain her putting her hand in my lap under the dinner table and getting within an inch of my dick before I managed to stop her?"

"Possibly she didn't know how close she was to the family jewels," Dylan argued weakly. He didn't really keep up with it, but he figured Claudia must be in her early twenties now. She was the picture of a California girl, with long blond hair, a year-round tan, and a tall, slim build.

"They were in the penthouse, and since the resort was booked, I ended up staying with them. Big mistake. She crawled in my bed the second night I was there and assured me that Mommy and Daddy couldn't hear anything. Oh, and I know where some of our money has gone. She's definitely got a new rack."

"Christ." Dylan grimaced. "That's so messed up. You didn't, right?"

Ash moved his foot to kick him on the shin. "Give me some credit here. I may not have many standards, but I have to stop short at family, even if they're not actually blood. I packed my shit and hit the road the next day. Since I'm a few days ahead of schedule, I thought I'd drop by here and see how things are on your end."

"Same ole," Dylan mumbled, not wanting to lay his sorta-relationship problems on his brother. Ash was the last one of his brothers who would understand something like that. In that regard, he and Dylan had always been similar. Though whereas Dylan avoided long-term commitments because he didn't really have time for them, Ash mainly did it because he couldn't imagine tying himself down to one woman—after Fiona. She'd done a real number on him, and Dylan wasn't sure that he'd ever recover from her betrayal.

"What about Zoe? Any progress in that area?" Ash asked idly, then his eyes widened as he took in Dylan's expression. *Dammit, stop looking guilty. He's never going to leave now.*

"Well, I'll be damned," he drawled as he sat up in his chair. "You actually went through with it. You slept with her."

"You know we don't need to share everything," Dylan grumbled. "I don't think she would want everyone around knowing that."

"It wasn't good, huh? Damn, that's too bad. But maybe good in a way too. At least you can go back to being friends and not be tempted to cross that line again. It's always disappointing to me when a woman appears to have so much potential, but couldn't get me off with a fucking roadmap and detailed instructions. And don't get me started on the bad head. How hard is it to suck a man's dick? It's not as if we're that picky. Just get down there and tap that inner Hoover. But no. Last week I slept with this gorgeous chick and she was a drooler. She went down on me and I had spit dripping down my legs afterward. Seriously, it was like Niagara Falls as she went at it. I had to force myself to come as quick as possible or risk an accidental drowning."

He couldn't help it. Dylan threw his head back and laughed. "That's disgusting, bro. Where in the world did you find such a winner?"

"Friend of a friend." He shrugged. "In hindsight, not a great idea. Now she keeps sending messages through him. That's the screwed-up part. People who are bad in bed never actually know it, which makes things even more awkward. I feel like I should send her a pity e-mail and detail exactly what the problem was. Maybe suggest she get a bib and a kiddie pool for her next victim."

"There's something seriously wrong with you," Dylan mocked. "How do you even come up with this shit?"

"Nothing to make up when it actually happened. Now, back to your predicament. I assume things are a tad strained between you and Zoe now. I hope you didn't promise her a new house, puppies, and unlimited Netflix. You did make it known up front that it was just sex, right?"

This was getting out of control fast. He didn't really want to talk to his brother about his sex life, but he couldn't have Ash assuming she was so horrible in bed that Dylan was looking for a way out. "Zoe and I are giving things a try between us. As a couple, I guess you could say. And she wasn't bad. Actually, it was the best I've ever had."

Ash blinked a few times as if processing his words. "Well, why didn't you lead with that? I even told you a painful story from my past so you'd feel better."

Rolling his eyes, Dylan said, "Because I happen to care about her and I don't want her embarrassed that everyone in the state knows we've had sex."

Ash gave him a blank look. Yeah, it was always hard for men to think like a woman. He'd certainly never bothered much before. But with Zoe he wanted to be better than the frat boy version of himself that he should have outgrown years ago. "I have no idea what you're talking about, but when you find your dick again, let me know. Anyway, how are things going with the whole relationship thing? You don't exactly look like you're walking on water."

Dylan had to draw the line somewhere. He didn't want to talk about last night again, especially with Ash. His brother would see nothing at all wrong with what had transpired. So he simply said, "Things are fine. It's been busy this morning and I was just going down to see her for a minute. Do you want me to call and have a room prepared for you first?"

Ash got to his feet and slung an arm around his shoulders. "Nope, I'll take care of that. Let's go down and see your sweet thang."

Shit. He had no idea how he was going to talk to Zoe with his brother along to watch their every move. The only positive he could see was that she might go easier on him in front of Ash. "Let's go," he sighed, knowing that Asher wouldn't miss this now. He had no idea why the man was his favorite brother, because sometimes he was simply a pain in the ass.

⁓

"Holy wet panties, Batgirl," hissed Dana as she froze. Zoe looked up to see what had her friend so riveted and felt her own heart skip a beat as Dylan slowly approached where they were standing. "Who is that stud with your man?" Dana whispered as she elbowed her in the side.

"Ouch," Zoe murmured. Truthfully, she'd only had eyes for Dylan, so she glanced at the other man for the first time. She hadn't seen him in quite a while, but Asher Jackson wasn't someone you'd ever forget. He had the same dark hair and coloring as Dylan, but his body was even more muscular. He reminded her of a sleek jaguar. There was a sense of barely suppressed power and animalistic beauty that immediately hit you in the face when you looked at him. He also had a great sense of humor, which she hadn't expected the first time they'd met. She knew that he teased Dylan about their friendship, so she wondered what he'd had to say about the change in their relationship—if Dylan had told him. "That's Asher, Dylan's brother," she whispered to Dana right before the two men stopped in front of them.

"Hey, sweetheart." Dylan surprised her with the endearment, especially in front of Asher. Apparently the other man did indeed know. She was further shocked when, without hesitation, he pulled her to his side and dropped a kiss onto her lips. *Okay. Not a shy bone in his body, even after last night. Interesting.* Maybe he had no intention of addressing what had happened, but she certainly didn't plan to let it go.

"Morning," she murmured and then turned to the other man. "Hi, Asher, it's good to see you again. I didn't know you were in town."

"Hey, gorgeous," Asher replied, grinning. "You look absolutely delicious this morning." Zoe knew she was blushing. How could you get a compliment like that from a man like Asher and not turn into a schoolgirl?

Dylan was glaring at his brother when Zoe said, "Er . . . thanks." Then Dana cleared her throat loudly, obviously wanting an introduction. "Oh, Asher, I'd like you to meet my friend Dana."

Asher stepped to the side so that he could see Dana, and Zoe was surprised to see something flicker in his eyes. Maybe she was imagining it, but there was a heavy current running between the two that was impossible to miss. When Dana extended her hand, Ash hesitated for a long moment before enfolding it between his own. "Pleasure," he said simply, then pulled away immediately. Turning abruptly to Dylan, he added, "Listen I'm going to go get set up in a room. I'm beat after the trip up. I'll touch base with you later on this evening. We'll all catch dinner or something." He glanced briefly at Zoe saying, "Later, gorgeous," before striding quickly from the shop.

That was weird, Zoe thought, then knew she wasn't the only one who felt that way when Dylan stood staring after his brother. Still looking perplexed over Ash's abrupt exit, he took her hand and asked, "Can we talk for a minute?" He glared at Dana, who remained where she was, also staring after the man who'd literally run from the room.

"Sure. Have a seat in the back and I'll bring us a snack." She walked behind the counter and fixed them both a cup of regular coffee with cream and sugar and put them on a tray along with some blueberry scones that her mother had dropped off earlier that morning. Zoe had missed breakfast so her stomach growled in anticipation as she made her way to where Dylan was sitting in the back corner. "Anything wrong with Ash?" she asked in concern. "He seemed fine until he shook hands with Dana, then it was as if he freaked out over something. They'd never even met so I don't think it was actually anything to do with her."

"I don't know what that was all about," he admitted. "He was looking forward to torturing us both so I'm not sure what could have caused him to give that up. I think we should just be grateful, though."

"So you told him about us, I assume," she guessed.

"I did," he confirmed. "I hope you don't mind. Ash is pretty astute so it's difficult to keep anything from him. You're okay with that, right?"

Settling in next to him, she smiled. "Sure, it's not like we've made a secret of it. My mother has probably told everyone including the postman and her hair dresser by now anyway." She hoped that he hadn't gone into detail about everything that had occurred between them, but she was happy that he was being open about the change in their relationship. That seemed like a good sign to her.

He took a sip of his coffee before clearing his throat. "I owe you a major apology for last night. I really don't even know where to start. I had no intention of staying when I left to get Josh. Then I found out I'd actually missed his birthday for the first time in years. I realize it sounds silly for grown men, but it's sorta always been a thing with my group of friends that we celebrate together. I know there's no excuse for it, but I simply got caught up in what was going on around me and I lost sight of what was actually important."

Putting a hand on his arm, Zoe said softly, "Josh came by earlier and told me his version of what happened. He felt like the whole thing was his fault. I assume you told him about everything this morning."

Dylan looked downright shocked. "Um, yeah. He called me and I was pretty short with him, even though it was all on me." He took her hand in his, bringing her fingers to his lips and kissing them. "Baby, you have no clue how shitty I felt about the whole thing this morning. I'm ashamed to admit this and I probably shouldn't because you may dump my ass, but I took a cab home and pretty much passed out. I'm so used to not having anyone waiting for me at home that it didn't even occur to me that you were gone until I woke up this morning. I can't believe I did that, Zoe."

She had to admit, that part stung a lot. She did have to give him credit for actually admitting to it, because she likely would have never known the difference. "I was angry at the time, but more than that, my feelings were hurt." Releasing a deep breath, she added, "but I've been your friend for a long time and I know that what we're doing is a different ballgame for you. It is for me as well. The only difference is that I don't have much of an active social life and you do. Which is fine. I'd never expect you to give that up for me. If you'd called and explained that you were staying, I would have been more than okay with it. But instead, hours passed and I didn't hear from you. I was afraid you'd been in an accident. Then when I did get you on the phone, I wasn't even sure you knew it was me."

Dylan closed his eyes briefly before opening them again. She could see the sincerity there as he said, "I promise that won't happen again."

When he opened his mouth to say more, she put a finger over his lips and shook her head. "That's all I need to hear. I don't want to make this into a huge deal. We've just started seeing each other as more than friends, and I have no interest in being the woman who brings nothing but drama to your life. Our relationship has always worked because we feel comfortable being ourselves with each other. I don't want to lose or change that. If you'd stood me up as friends, I'd have given you a little hell and moved on. Same thing here. It's only a big thing if we make it into one, which I'm not. Does that work for you?"

"God, I want you," Dylan growled as he dropped a

hand beneath the table and ran it up her thigh. "You're incredible and I'm so hard right now my dick is digging into my zipper. Can we please go to your office again?"

"No way!" Zoe laughed. *Yes, yes!* "I'd never hear the end of it if my mother decided to drop by again."

"Thanks for that, babe. Mentioning your mother took care of my hard-on."

"Awe," she cooed, "I bet I can get that back for you tonight. Do you think you'll be able to get away from the office at a decent time? I'll cook dinner and you can have me for dessert."

"I'll make it happen," he promised and she knew that he would regardless of what he had to cancel to do it. That was one thing about Dylan—he'd never failed to make it up to her when something interfered with their plans. They got to their feet and shared a brief kiss before he left. As she got back to work, she couldn't help thinking that she was officially one of those women who felt like all was right in their world when things were going well with the man they loved. Sappy, certainly. But after years of trying to get her man to notice her, she felt like she had a lot of lost time to make up for and she intended to experience everything that she'd missed and then some.

Fourteen

Dylan arrived at Zoe's with ten minutes to spare. There was no way in hell he'd have been late, regardless of what he had to juggle to get there at all. He'd canceled a dinner meeting and a conference call, but she was more important. She'd been so decent about the whole mess from last night that it had made him appreciate the woman that she was all over again. It seemed crazy to him now that he'd spent so much time not seeing her as anything other than a friend. It wasn't her makeover that had brought him to his senses, although that had certainly sped up the process. It was the thoughts of losing her to another man. As long as she wasn't dating, then there was no one there to take her away from him. He'd come to accept that possibly Ash was right. In his mind she had always been his. He didn't think he'd have ever been able to see her end up with anyone else.

Speaking of Ash, Dylan had flat out told him that he'd be spending the night with her and he'd have to find something else to do. Of course, Ash, being Ash, had been more than happy to hit a local bar and find his own entertainment for the evening. Dylan preferred not to think of what that would be.

He knocked on the door and Zoe opened it immediately as if she'd been waiting for him. His eyes almost bugged out of his head when he saw her standing there in a thin T-shirt and, from the looks of it, nothing else. She waved him inside, closing the door behind him. She took both of his hands in hers, looking at him excitedly. "I want to try something right now if you're willing."

Grinning at her enthusiasm, he said, "Sure, sweetheart. What'd you have in mind?"

He'd expected her to hit him up to watch another chick flick, which of course, he would agree to—he always did. So when she whispered near his ear, "I want to give my first blowjob if you'll let me," he almost went to his knees.

Maybe I imagined that. "Um . . . did you say . . . ?"

"Blowjob," she repeated. "It's probably not going to be very good, but I've been reading some of those step-by-step tutorials, plus I watched one in a porn movie a few minutes ago. They make everything look so easy, though. I'm sure it's harder in real life. You can help out by telling me what you like and what you don't. I'll get better at it," she said earnestly. *So fucking adorable and hot.*

"Babe, if you don't stop talking about it, I'm going to come in my pants. I'd be thrilled to receive your first blow job, so by all means, lead the way. You're running the show."

She beamed at him before saying, "Okay, if you'll go to the bedroom, I'll be there in a minute. I just need to get something really quick. You can go ahead and take your clothes off if you want to. Wait, would you rather I did that?"

Biting his tongue to keep from laughing, he shook his head. "I'll take care of it." He walked down the hallway and into her room. She'd left both bedside lamps on so the space was dimly lit with a warm glow. The speed with which he removed his clothing said a lot about his eagerness to experience what was to come. Knowing he was the first man that she'd ever had in her mouth was making him crazy. He took a few deep breaths to regain control and wondered what was taking her so long. He was standing in the middle of the floor with his hands on his hips and his dick hard against his stomach when she appeared in the doorway holding a bowl in one hand and a cup in the other. *What in the hell?* Maybe he should have told her that a blowjob didn't actually require anything other than her mouth and possibly her hand. "What do you have there, sweetheart?"

Instead of answering him, she said, "Could you come to the side of the bed and lie down?" He hesitated for a moment before moving to comply with her request. He'd promised to let her have control, so he needed to go with it. Ash's description of his disaster blowjob ran through his head, but he pushed it aside. However, Zoe's touch would feel good; he didn't doubt that. So he lay down on the bed and kept his eyes to the ceiling as she set her items on the nearby table. "If you'll close your eyes, this will feel better." *Shit, this is getting weird.* But he did as she asked and tried to keep an open mind. The bed shifted as she climbed up next to him, then he felt her hands wrap around his cock and any further thought was impossible.

She stroked him firmly from root to tip, then rubbed her finger across the precum gathering at the head. "Feels amazing, baby," he praised. Then he was in her mouth and it was heaven. She licked and sucked him better than he'd ever had it before. Then she was gone. "What?" Oh dear God, then she was back and her mouth was so hot, it was as if his dick was sliding through velvet lava. "Fuck!" he hissed as he fisted her hair. "That's amazing." Again, she shifted away, and in another few seconds, his cock was surrounded by what felt like ice. His hips thrust as the difference between the hot and cold pushed him over the edge with little warning. "Zoe, I'm coming," he yelled as he attempted to pull back. It was her first time and he didn't want to assume that she would want a mouthful of come. But she refused to loosen her grip and he couldn't stop. He was dimly aware that she was taking everything he had to give. Some women refused to swallow, which even though it was hot as hell when they did, he certainly understood if it wasn't their thing. That Zoe would want to do that for him so soon was strangely touching.

He lay there boneless and sated as he attempted to catch his breath. It was the best blowjob he'd ever had, hands down. When he was able to focus, he looked up to see her kneeling beside him, looking uncertain. "Was it okay? I read that the hot-cold thing really felt good for a guy and I wanted to do something special for you."

Reaching out, he put a hand on her thigh, saying sincerely, "Sweetheart, you rocked my world. That was phenomenal. I thought I'd have a heart attack a few times, but holy shit, it was amazing."

"Really?" she asked, looking hopeful. "Was there anything that you'd like for me to do differently next time?"

"Hell no." He shook his head fervently. "Don't change a thing. You were perfect." They shared a long kiss before her stomach growling interrupted the moment. He laughed softly and swatted her ass. "Up with you. I'm going to clean up and then we'll eat dinner and I'll have you the entire night afterward."

As she scampered away, he felt an unexpected pang in his heart. Had he wasted years when he'd had the perfect one for him by his side all along? He had to marvel at the ease at which they'd transitioned from friends to something more. Both of them danced around the title at times, but if this wasn't a real relationship, he didn't know what was. They may have only officially changed the nature of it a few days ago, but a part of him knew that it had really started years ago when he'd first lain eyes on the dark-haired beauty who would come to be his world in every meaning of the word.

Fifteen

Zoe clicked the End button on her cell phone and tossed it on her desk. She and Dylan had made plans to have dinner and see a movie tonight, but he'd just canceled. She was disappointed, but she'd tried not to let it show. She knew he was doing the best that he could, but the constant pressures of his job, especially with the expansion plans moving ahead, were dimming some of the new relationship glow for her. She didn't want to come off as one of those clingy females who gave up all her own interests when she had a man in her life, but she did want to spend some quality time with him doing couple things.

Blowing out a breath of resignation, she took the inventory sheet that Dana had placed on her desk earlier and decided to go ahead and put next week's order together before she left. There was no reason to rush home now.

She had no idea how long she'd been sitting at her desk when she heard a knock on the door. Figuring it was one of the nighttime servers with a question, she called out, "Come in." Her eyes widened with shock when she saw Josh standing there smiling at her. He'd become somewhat of a regular in the shop since she and Dylan had been officially dating. And even though he always said the right things, something about him still made her uncomfortable. She could tell that Dylan wasn't really thrilled about his friend coming in that often either, and had asked her to let him know if he said anything out of line. So far that hadn't been the case. "Um . . . Josh, what are you doing here?" she asked in confusion. Suddenly on alert, she sat forward. "Is Dylan okay?"

Waving a hand casually around, Josh gave her a smile that looked almost predatory. "Oh, sure, he's fine, Zoe. We've had plans to grab a drink a few times, but he's had to bail on me. I guess work is taking over his life even more than usual right now. I probably don't need to tell you that, though."

Grimacing, she shook her head in commiseration. "No, I figured that out on my own. It'll get better, though, when this expansion is finished. Until then, this is his life."

Zoe shifted uncomfortably when Josh moved from the doorway and took one of the chairs in front of her desk. She might see him more now than she ever had before, but in her mind, that didn't make them friends. And her office wasn't exactly roomy. She felt as if he was invading her space, but she was clueless as to what to do about it. She should have made a point to say that she was busy before he took a seat. "So how've you been doing?"

"Er . . . good," she replied as she prayed that one of her employees would interrupt her. It went against her nature to be rude, but this whole situation was beginning to feel awkward. It wasn't necessarily what he said; it was the way he was looking at her as if he could see through her clothes. *You're just imagining it. This is one of Dylan's best friends. He wouldn't violate the whole bro-code, right?*

Good manners had her asking, "And you?"

He shrugged, then shot her a grin. "Can't complain. Of course, if I had a woman like you, I sure wouldn't leave her hanging to sit in an office all night. That little assistant of his might be a hot number, but she's got nothing on you, sweetheart. She's also a rude bitch."

Zoe's mouth dropped open at his harsh words about Lisa. Dylan's assistant stopped in most mornings for coffee and Zoe had always liked her. She also knew that Lisa was a hard worker who didn't take any shit from her boss, something that Dylan respected a lot. "Josh," she said firmly. "I don't think this is appropriate—"

Before she could finish, he cut her off. "You're a nice girl and I know you don't want to insult anyone. That's one thing I like about you. I've never been with anyone who didn't have an agenda. You're beautiful. I mentioned that, right?"

Holy shit, what is going on with him? This was officially the weirdest conversation that she'd had lately and that was saying something. This whole encounter didn't feel right. He'd said some stuff that was out of line, but it was his behavior that was bothering her the most. He almost appeared to be high. His feet were drumming against her floor and he'd been fidgeting in his seat the entire time. There was a restless energy emitting from him that was putting her on edge. She wanted him gone—now. Zoe was in the process of getting to her feet when her barista Jill walked in. "Hey, Zoe. Oops, I didn't know you had company."

"No!" she shrilled out, before lowering her voice. "I mean, that's fine. What did you need?"

Jill looked at her strangely before saying, "The cooler where we store the juice and whipped cream is making a loud noise. Thought you should know about it."

Zoe was around her desk in seconds. "I'll check it right now. We don't want to lose everything in it if it goes out overnight." She glanced at Josh, then looked quickly away when she found him staring at her. "I've got to get back to work, Josh."

She waited impatiently for him to get to his feet, then found herself once again as the recipient of an unwanted hug. This time she made no pretense of returning the embrace. She didn't want to encourage him. He pulled away and said, "I'll see you soon, Zoe."

God, I hope not, Zoe thought as she followed Jill behind the counter. Maybe she was on edge because she was tired and disappointed that her date was canceled. But something just didn't seem right with Josh, and she vowed to avoid him if at all possible in the future. She'd mention it to Dylan as well. She knew he wouldn't be happy about his friend's comments concerning his assistant. She pushed the incident from her mind as she called the repairman and helped Jill and Meg with the evening crowd. By the time she was home, she'd managed to convince herself that it hadn't been nearly as strange as she'd thought it was at the time.

⤫

Dylan rolled his eyes at Ash across the table as Hal, the contractor for their expansion project, droned on and on. He'd been forced to cancel his evening with Zoe to deal with yet another crisis. And now that the issue had been resolved, he was ready to go home. Fuck, was an early night occasionally too much to ask?

He wanted to get up and applaud when Ash released

a long sigh and snapped out, "Hal, man, is there a point to this story or not? Because I'm about to fall face-first in my dessert plate over here."

The other man paused before roaring with laughter. "Damned if I know." He shook his head before slapping Dylan on the back. "I guess I better get out of here anyway. The wife will be pissed that I'm getting home so late again. You know how that goes."

"Not really." Ash shrugged before raising his hand and signaling the nearby server for their check. "We'll take care of this, Hal. Why don't you head on out before you get in trouble?"

They all shook hands before agreeing to meet at the office the next afternoon to look over the new blueprints. "Thanks, brother," Dylan muttered as Ash signed the credit card slip in front of him. "I didn't think he was ever going to shut up."

Ash gave him a knowing grin before saying, "You're just cranky because you had to miss your date. I could have handled this tonight. Hell, it didn't turn out to be anything major anyway."

Rubbing the bridge of his nose, Dylan said, "It's my job. Yeah, it sucks that I'm constantly breaking plans with my girlfriend, but surely things will settle down once this expansion is finished."

"It'll be like it always is," Ash began. "Things will be smooth for a few days, then something will happen. If Zoe can't deal with that, then you've got a problem.

These resorts have always been our girlfriends, wives, and children. We give them everything we've got and sometimes there's damn little left over for anything else."

"You don't have to tell me that," Dylan snapped. "I've been on the front lines for as long as you have. And Zoe never complains about my schedule. Hell, I think I'd feel better if she did because I know I'm a shitty boyfriend most of the time."

"That's exactly why I don't do complications," Ash pointed out. "Expectations and disappointments are a bitch to deal with. Give a woman an hour of bliss and she'll thank you. Put a pretty title on it and bail on dinner, then see what happens." When Dylan only stared at him, Ash sighed. "Listen, I'm not trying to be an asshole. I know you care about her. Hell, I believe I pointed it out while you still had your head in your ass over the whole thing. I'm not saying that you need to dump her. Just cut yourself some slack. She knows you better than most anyone else. It's not as if your life is some big mystery to her. She's accustomed to the hours you work. Yes, it's worse than ever right now, but the dust will settle a bit after we're finished with the expansion. Until then, shit like tonight is gonna happen. She's a big girl, and if she reaches her limit, she'll tell you. Otherwise, do the best you can and stop acting like such a chick all the time."

Dylan collapsed back in his chair and started laughing.

"I'm not sure why I talk to you about anything. You really are a dick."

"Absolutely," Ash agreed. "But I'm not eating Rolaids like candy and crying for my mommy." They both shuddered at the mention of their parental figure. "Um . . . forget I added that last part."

"Agreed," Dylan nodded. "Now if you don't mind, I'd like to go sleep beside my girlfriend for a few hours until we start all over again."

"That's the most depressing thing I've ever heard," Ash deadpanned. "Sleep has no place in the bedroom."

Dylan shook his head as they left the restaurant. Secretly, he had to agree. One of these nights he'd actually make it home while Zoe was still awake. *Fuck my life.*

Sixteen

"All dressed up and nowhere to go again, huh?" Dana asked sympathetically.

Zoe gave her a wry smile as she tossed her cell phone back into her purse. "That's life when you date the big man," she replied, attempting a feeble joke. In truth, it shouldn't have been much of a surprise to her that Dylan stayed so busy. Maybe a part of her had hoped that he'd be able to carve out a little more time in his schedule for her, and she knew that he tried, but there were only so many hours in the day. They'd been together for almost three months now, and other than feeling like ships that passed in the night at times, it had been amazing. They had settled into the relationship as if they'd been born to be partners. On the nights when he worked late, she'd wake up to find that he'd come to her place and crashed beside her at some point. It wasn't a perfect situation, but just seeing him lying there the next morning made her absurdly grateful that he was trying.

"It still sucks, though," Dana pointed out. "But luckily for you, I have no plans for the evening, so we're going out. How about a drink at Breakers? It's a new place right on the beach. I'll even buy you one of those cute little umbrella drinks."

Her first inclination was to refuse the offer and head home, but then she thought why not? She needed to have a life outside of Dylan, and sitting at home watching television for another night didn't sound appealing. Which was funny considering not long ago that had been her nightly routine. But Dylan had changed that somewhat, and she had no desire to go back to the Zoe of before. So plastering on a bright smile, she said, "You've got yourself a date. Let's lock up and get out of here."

Dana gave her a high five and they quickly shut off the lights in the shop and left the hotel. Dana volunteered to drive, promising only to have a glass of wine. If that changed, they could always call a taxi later. The new bar was less than five miles from the resort and Zoe had to admit that it had a lot of character. There were tons of smaller tables situated against a solid wall of glass facing the ocean. And if you were in the mood to be outdoors, there was plenty of seating there as well, along with volleyball courts for those who wanted to do more than sit. Obviously the locals and tourists loved it because the place was packed. Eighties rock blared inside as people stood in crowds talking, while some danced to the beat. "Let's go outside," Dana yelled out. Normally Zoe would have preferred to stay where there was air-conditioning, but a cool front had passed through a few days earlier, making the humidity almost nonexistent.

They grabbed a table that someone was in the process of vacating and ordered glasses of wine. "This tastes so good," Zoe moaned as she sipped the merlot. "I owe you for dragging me out tonight. I've already caught up on all the *Golden Girls* reruns, so tonight I'd have been starting *Seinfeld*."

Dana pretended to wipe a tear away. "That's so sad. He may be an ass sometimes, but you're dating one of the hottest men in the state. You should never even turn your television on, much less be watching marathons of old shows."

Zoe shrugged. "You know how busy he is. It's not his fault that I don't have some hobbies to keep me busy. Plus, I work late most evenings as well so what can I really say about him doing the same?"

"But you always make time for him," Dana pointed out. "Don't get me wrong, I know it must be a big job to run a resort like the Oceanix, but it's never going to get easier. Have you thought about that? Unless Dylan makes some changes, like hiring someone to help him, then this is your life forever. Sure, there'll be times when he has a break here and there, but understand in the years ahead that he's going to be an absent husband and father a lot of the time."

Zoe's laugh was strained as she attempted to lighten the effect that the other woman's words were having on her. "We are nowhere close to being married, much less having kids. And of course I know Dylan has a hectic schedule. Remember I've been friends with him since we were kids. It's not exactly a newsflash to me."

"Yeah, but you weren't dating him then. I'm not trying to be negative, but even though you're the happiest I've ever seen you, it's also impossible to miss the way your face falls when he calls or texts to let you know that he's either held up or can't make it at all. He's a good guy and you two are perfect for each other, but I just think you're making all the sacrifices here, and as long as you're willing to do that, what incentive does he have to change?"

Zoe slumped in her seat and gave up defending the man that she loved. It was actually a relief to talk to someone about it. "I feel crappy for complaining, but I miss him. Even when we're together at night, he's just a body in the same room with me. And I don't have the heart to tell him how I feel because he does try really hard to make time for me. With the expansion plans for the resort moving ahead, it's worse than ever. I can't imagine how it's going to be when they actually break ground soon. I went by his office last night to surprise him with dinner and he was asleep on his desk with his cell phone in one hand and a set of blueprints in the other."

Dana put a hand over hers, giving it a squeeze. "Oh, honey, I knew all this had to be getting to you. And even though I'm usually one to charge ahead and think later, I also understand why you're hesitant to tell him how this is making you feel, even though you're dead wrong about it."

Giving voice to her fears, Zoe admitted, "I'm afraid he'll say that we should go back to being friends. This isn't simply a job for him, it's his family business. He's not going to walk away from it and I wouldn't want that. But unfortunately, now that I know how good we are together, I want more. Even a meal or two a week where he's not spending half of his time on the phone or with his computer sitting on the table while he reviews a proposal."

"That man loves you, Zoe. You may think that you're the only one whose heart has been involved over the years, but he's invested as well. In true guy fashion, it might have taken him longer to realize it, but it's there. He's not going to be able to downgrade to a platonic relationship with you, and I know he doesn't want to lose you. So talk to him. It's not as if you're issuing some kind of ultimatum. You're simply letting him know where you stand and that you want more time together."

"You make it sound so easy," Zoe murmured as she stared into her now empty glass. "I don't want to add more stress to his life. He has enough for ten people already."

"But you have to be a priority too. I know he isn't neglecting you intentionally, but he needs to see that this is hard for you both. Just think about it." Zoe opened her mouth to respond when Dana suddenly whispered, "Incoming."

"What?" she asked in confusion before feeling a hand on her shoulder.

"Zoe! I thought that was you," boomed a voice that had become all too familiar. Dana gave her a grimace of distaste as Josh circled around to stand in front of their table. This was the first time she'd seen him since he'd popped into her office unexpectedly a few weeks earlier. She hadn't mentioned it to Dylan because he stayed so stressed that she didn't want to upset him if she was making something out of nothing.

"Hey, Josh," she said uneasily. "I didn't see you when we came in. It's so crowded, though, that would have probably been difficult." Without invitation, he pulled the chair out next to her and lowered himself onto it.

"Yeah, this is the new cool place in town. I was just

having a drink with some buddies. You're both welcome to join us if you'd like."

"We're leaving shortly," Dana tossed out. "We were having a little *girl* time after work." If Dana thought Josh would catch the emphasis she put on the "girl" part, she was sadly mistaken.

"That's cool. I'll keep you two company until you leave. Don't want any of those freaks messing with the prettiest women here." Dana made a gagging motion when he turned his head away that had Zoe biting her lip to keep a straight face. "Hey, where's Dylan? Still tied up with the new project?"

"He had a meeting with the city zoning board. He's trying to avoid any delays, but it's always something," she added lightly. The last thing she wanted was for Josh to run to Dylan before they talked and tell him she was whining about his work schedule.

Josh studied her carefully—which was more than a little unnerving. Finally, he said, "You and I have known Dylan for a long time. He's always been a go-getter, even in college. We put him in charge of damn near every event because we knew he'd kick ass until he made it happen. He's an ambitious SOB—which makes him good at everything he touches. Doesn't leave much for you, though, does it?"

Don't let him see he got to you. Zoe wanted to kiss her friend's feet when Dana stood up, yawning loudly. "Damn, I'm beat. Sorry to be the party pooper, but this girl needs to get home." Grabbing Zoe's arm, she pulled her up from the table. "Good to see you again, Jack," she added, no doubt intentionally messing up his name.

"Bye, Josh," Zoe threw over her shoulder as Dana propelled them across the sand and back through the packed bar. "God, thank you," Zoe hissed as they got in the car.

"I swear that dude is a real creeper." Dana shuddered. "I don't like the way he keeps popping up everywhere now. He's like your stalker or something."

Laughing, Zoe said, "We have a lot of people who come into the shop way more than he does. Plus, his best friend owns the resort, so it stands to reason he'd be around some."

"The guy wants in your pants, sister," Dana said bluntly. "And he's not above trashing Dylan to do it."

Zoe wrinkled her nose in disgust. "That's gross. There's no way that's happening, even if I wasn't with Dylan."

"Just be careful around him. I've known guys like that before and he's far from the harmless, good-time boy he tries to make himself out to be."

Trying to look more confident than she felt, Zoe shrugged. "It'll be fine." She'd told Dana about him making her uncomfortable in her office and Dana had warned her not to underestimate him. She was beginning to see that the other woman might be right. She'd avoid Josh until things calmed down with the expansion, then she'd take her concerns to Dylan.

∽

It was almost midnight when Dylan got to Zoe's. He let himself in the door quietly, then promptly removed his coat and tie before unbuttoning his shirt. His body was beyond exhausted, but his mind was going a mile a minute as it often did after a long day. He stopped at the hallway closet and kicked his shoes off before going to the kitchen to get a bottle of water.

His life was always hectic, but this last month had been a whole different animal as the new construction moved from the planning to the execution stage. Despite his best intentions, there were still problems, delays, and a shitload of red tape to be dealt with on a daily basis. He had moments when he didn't know how he was going to manage a project so big. The Oceanix Resorts in Florida were by far the most profitable, and his location did more business than all the others. Without Lisa working equally long hours, he'd probably have sunk long ago. But he knew that, at some point, changes would have to be made. When Lisa eventually decided to start a family, she couldn't continue to pull the responsibility she was dealing with. Shit, just thinking about it made his head hurt.

All he wanted to do was go curl up with Zoe and enjoy some stolen moments with the woman he adored.

Their time together lately had been far too short and he hated himself for letting her down so often. The fact that she was always so gracious about it almost made it worse. Hell, he'd have felt better if she'd cussed him out. No one liked or deserved to be neglected and he knew that's what he was doing. Truthfully, he'd known all along that he didn't have time for a relationship. Sex here and there, yeah, most men would find a way to make that happen. But she was so much more than that to him. Even Ash had been sympathetic when he'd mentioned it to him earlier. He'd been frustrated as hell over bailing on their plans yet again, and it had come pouring out after he'd snapped his brother's head off a few times. "I know you don't want to hear it, bro, but it's the nature of the beast," Ash had said. "I'm not saying it can't work, because Seth has managed to do it. But you're going to have to be willing to change the way you've always lived your life."

"I thought I already had," he'd joked weakly. "I'm in a real relationship for the first time in my adult life."

"Yeah, you are. But are you prepared to do whatever it takes to keep it? Because if you're not, then you should throw in the towel now before anyone gets hurt."

He'd mulled those words over long after he'd ended the call with Ash. He didn't have any answers or even suggestions at this point, knowing what the construction period at the resort would be like, but he knew that he needed to talk to Zoe. If for no other reason than to let her know he was aware he'd been a shitty boyfriend lately. Together he had to believe that they could come up with a way to make it work. He knew they'd promised to remain friends regardless, but he didn't want to go back to that because when he'd made that agreement, he hadn't understood how much he'd come to love having her in his arms at night. The feel of her breath on his chest and the steady thump of her heartbeat lulled him to sleep when nothing else in the world could.

Seventeen

Zoe rolled over, then smiled in sleepy contentment as she felt the warm weight at her back. Dylan had shown up after she'd gone to bed last night. She loved that he'd been doing that so often lately. She knew that he probably had to get up soon, but she didn't go into the shop until noon today so there was time to enjoy her man.

She pulled out of his arms and grinned when he shifted onto his back, tossing an arm over his head. The sheet was barely covering his obviously hard dick, if the tent around it was any indication. She'd been thrilled to know that the myth of morning wood was actually very much a truth. And today she planned to take advantage of it. So she edged the sheet down slowly, careful not to wake him up. She studied him for a moment, thinking he was the most beautiful man she'd ever seen. His thick lashes lay against his cheeks like crescents. His full mouth, which brought her so much pleasure, felt as if it was made for hers. And those insane abs—so completely and utterly lickable. On the days he didn't make it to the gym, he did an insane amount of sit-ups. His thighs were firmly muscled from years of running on the beach. And his dick—oh, how she wished she could write songs and poetry about that delicious body part.

It had been a while since she'd given him her first blowjob, but it certainly never got old. She loved having him in her mouth almost as much as she enjoyed him going down on her. Just the thought of it had moisture pooling between her thighs. Shooting him a quick glance to make sure he was still asleep, she gently closed her hand around his thick length and pumped up and down a few times. His dick jerked in her hold and she held her breath, thinking surely he'd wake up any moment, but so far he was blissfully unaware of what she was doing—well, maybe one part of him was.

She leaned down, running her tongue across his tip before opening wider to take him in. Her hands and mouth worked in sync as he grew impossibly hard. Without thinking, she lowered her other hand and began stroking her clit, needing a release as well. She was completely lost in obtaining pleasure for both of them when a voice said, "Fuck, that's the hottest thing I've ever seen."

Zoe jerked so hard that she was afraid she'd damn near pulled his dick off as he yelled. "Shit, I'm so sorry. Are you okay? You shouldn't have scared me like that Dylan, God!"

For a moment, she thought he was crying as his big body shook. Then she got a good look at his face and knew it was laughter. "I'm fine, babe, but if you'd been a bit stronger, this could have ended very differently."

"You ass." She rolled her eyes, then found herself giggling as well.

"I wish I'd kept my mouth shut, because I liked what you were doing down there," he added ruefully.

Feeling bold, Zoe carefully tossed a leg over his legs and moved until she was hovering just inches over his still hard cock. "Let me know how you feel about this, then," she purred as she lowered herself inch by inch until she'd taken him all. After a clean bill of health for both of them, Zoe had gone on birth control so condoms were no longer necessary. She hadn't thought she would notice a difference, but the feel of Dylan bare was so much different. He'd never been inside a woman without a condom, so it was a first that made her feel special.

"God damn," he groaned, "that's amazing, baby." She rocked back and forth as he lifted his hips to meet her on each downward stroke. "So good," he praised as his hands guided her movements. It was a slow and leisurely loving that neither of them appeared to be in a hurry to end. She ground against his root, while he sucked one of her nipples into his mouth. The feel of his teeth nipping the sensitive bud had her right on the edge.

"Dylan," she moaned, "I'm so close." He released her other nipple with a pop before sliding his hand between her thighs to rub her clit. Then she was coming apart in his arms as her orgasm worked its way through her entire body. He held her upright and buried himself deep one last time before emptying into her.

They both lay panting beside each other with Dylan drawing lazy circles on her thigh. "I'm pretty sure you're going to kill me one day, but I'm willing to risk it." He gently turned her face toward his and kissed her slowly and thoroughly.

"I wish we could stay here forever," Zoe sighed as she laid her head on his chest.

"Me too, sweetheart," he murmured. Then, clearing his throat, he surprised her by saying, "I wanted to talk to you and now seems like a good time since we actually have a few minutes to ourselves."

"Okay," she replied warily. *Surely he wouldn't break up with me after sex.*

"First off, I'm sorry about last night. And I hate that it seems like I'm constantly apologizing now for being late or canceling plans."

"Honey, I know things are crazy for you right now," Zoe responded automatically. *Shut up and let him talk. Stop panicking.*

"They are," he agreed. "I wish I could say that it'll be better soon, but you know as well as I do that my life isn't ever calm for long. With this expansion, it's going to get much worse before I see anything approaching better." He turned on his side and she did the same until they were facing each other. "If I wasn't such a selfish bastard, I'd let you go, but I can't do that." She felt some of the fear that had been threatening to choke her dissipate at his words. *Thank God.* "I'm asking you to please be patient with me while I try to figure something out. I can't make you any promises because I don't know what's going to happen, but I'm trying, I really am." Then he added, "I love you, Zoe," so quietly that she missed it at first.

"Wh-what did you say?" *Please don't let me have heard him wrong.*

He trailed a finger down her cheek, then across her parted lips. "I love you. I've always loved you. It took me a while to figure out that it hadn't been as just a friend in a long time."

"Oh, Dylan, I love you too, and have forever," she confessed. "I've known for a while that it was more than friendship for me. I could only hope that you'd feel the same at some point."

"I'm sorry I was slow to find my way," he said tenderly,

"but I'm here with you now and I never want to leave." They both laughed as no sooner had those last words left his mouth than his phone rang. "Shit, I jinxed myself," he grumbled.

Zoe kissed the corner of his mouth before rolling to the edge of the bed and getting up. "I'm going to take a shower. Go get 'em, tiger." When she reached the bathroom, she hugged herself as she fought the urge to squeal in happiness. *He loves me.* She was so close to having everything that she'd ever wanted, it was almost scary. He was also going to work on finding a way for them to have more time together. What more could she ask of him? Regardless of how hectic things got, she couldn't imagine a circumstance that would make her walk away from him. Little did she know that within days she would come to question everything she'd always thought she wanted.

Eighteen

"Thanks for bringing me dinner again, sweetheart," Dylan said as he kissed her neck. After the shop had closed at nine, she'd fixed a plate for both of them and took the elevator up to see him. As he'd predicted, things were almost insane with the construction date getting closer and closer. She'd promised to be patient, though, and she was sticking by that. Stolen moments such as these were both precious and necessary to keep the lines of communication open in their relationship.

She was sitting in his lap, dreading going home alone once again. "I'm just glad we got to see each other for a few minutes. You're staying at your place tonight, right?" She knew he had an early breakfast meeting across town as well as a conference call so it didn't make sense to drive to her condo at midnight, only to come back here within a few hours.

"Yeah, I guess so," he answered glumly. "I'll miss you, though. Sure you don't want to pack a bag and stay with me?"

"I'm not opening tomorrow so I promised Mom I'd take Dolly to the vet." Before he could answer, a phone icon on his laptop began buzzing and she knew it was Ash and the rest of the brothers for their daily status update call. She could tell that he was already distracted when she kissed his cheek and got to her feet. "Call me later if you get a moment."

"I will, babe," he agreed automatically, before hitting a button on his computer and connecting the call. Zoe sighed and took her purse from the corner of his desk.

It was after ten when she walked through the employee parking lot to her car. She fastened her seat belt and started the engine before backing out of her space and pulling out onto the main road. In another mile she turned off onto a side street that she'd taken to using because it was much quieter than the tourist areas.

She was halfway home when she heard a popping sound before her steering wheel began jerking. *Shit, what in the hell?* she thought frantically as she fought to keep the car on the road while slowing her speed. Her heart was racing and her hands were shaking when she finally managed to pull to the side of the road. She put the car in Park and sat there for a moment, trying to calm herself. The area around here was deserted, with the nearest house probably two miles away. She opened her purse and fumbled through it looking for her phone. *No, no.* She cried out as she emptied the small bag onto the front seat. Where was her phone? She thought back and remembered having it in the kitchen when she'd called Dylan to see what he wanted for dinner. Dear God, she must have left it there. Maybe she could drive the car far enough to get help. She took her flashlight from the glove box and opened the door. A quick inspection revealed that her front left tire was flat. The rubber was sitting right on the rim, which she knew was a bad thing. She absolutely shouldn't drive it, but what choice did she have?

Zoe was weighing her options when she saw lights in the distance. Excitedly she ran to the back of the car, thinking she'd flag them down. Then she froze. What if it was some psycho? She was on a deserted street alone. Maybe she should hide instead. Before she could decide, the car was upon her and slowing. She stepped back as they pulled to within inches of her bumper before stopping. She swallowed audibly as their door opened and a tall figure came toward her. "Zoe? Is that you?"

"Josh." She sagged in relief. What were the odds of it actually being someone she knew? "I'm so glad to see you. My tire blew out and I left my phone at the shop. Could I use yours to call someone?"

He stopped at her side, giving her a concerned look. "Of course, but why don't I take you home? A friend of mine runs a garage, so I can give him a call and have him come pick your car up and fix it. It's too deserted for you to be out here any longer than absolutely necessary."

"That would be great," she agreed. "I'd love a ride. I don't live far from here, so I hope it's not out of your way."

He opened the passenger-side door of his Porsche for her, then crossed to the other side to get in. "Where's Dylan at tonight? He shouldn't let you drive by yourself in this kind of area."

"He's working," Zoe sighed. It seemed like she repeated that same thing to someone at least ten times a day. You'd think by now they'd already know the answer before they bothered to ask the question. Josh pulled onto the road, then put a hand on the gearshift. Zoe had been so lost in her thoughts that she jumped in surprise when she felt something on her leg. She looked down in shock to see his hand there, inching up toward the apex of her thighs. "What do you think you're doing?" she asked incredulously as she attempted to pry his fingers lose.

"You don't have to pretend anymore, baby. We've been hot for each other since that night at my party. I know you feel obligated to Dylan because you're friends, and that's cool. He's my buddy too. He doesn't need to know what we do in our private time. Fuck, he's probably getting sucked off by that assistant of his right now."

"Get your hands off me!" she cried as she felt him inches away from her underwear. Why had she worn a dress today of all days? His foot was heavy on the gas pedal and Zoe felt completely out of control as he spewed more insanity about them being together. She made one last attempt to dislodge his hand before he touched her intimately and realized her mistake too late. He was so engrossed in what was happening on the other side of the car that his eyes had left the road. She cried out a warning as she saw the approaching curve, but it was too late. The last thing she remembered was the feeling of weightlessness as the car flew through the air and into the unknown. *Dylan.*

တ

It was close to one in the morning when Dylan turned off the light to his office and walked down the hallway to the elevator. The double doors were opening and he was stepping on when his phone rang. *What now?* he thought wearily. He was tempted to turn the damn thing off, but that was never really an option for him. He stared at it in shock when he saw Vivian's name on the screen. In a split second, he knew. God, no. *Zoe.* "Don't you dare tell me something's happened to her," he growled in way of a greeting.

Vivian, as always in times of crisis, was direct and

to the point. "Dylan, she's going to be all right, but you need to get to Southside Hospital right now. I'll tell you everything when you get here. Make sure you do it in one piece." With that, she ended the call and he was left staring at the screen. Then he jolted into action and ran into the elevator before frantically punching the button for the parking garage. After that, he had no recollection of driving to the hospital. It was all a blur until he pulled into the fire lane and left his car, along with the keys, there. He couldn't give a shit if someone stole or towed it away.

"Zoe Hart," he snapped when he reached the emergency room check-in area.

"Dylan, over here," Vivian called out, waving him to a small seating area in the corner.

"What's going on?" he asked as he pushed his shaking hands in his pockets. "Where is she? You said she was all right."

"Sit down, Dylan," she snapped, and he automatically complied. "Now get it together. She's going to need you."

"Please," he pleaded, needing to know where the woman he loved more than life was.

Vivian softened, putting a comforting hand on his arm. "She was in a car accident." When he opened his mouth to respond, she stopped him with a shake of her head. "Let me finish. She's okay, believe me. I would tell you if she wasn't." He nodded his agreement and she continued. "Dylan, the police are involved as well. When Zoe's tire blew out, she realized she'd left her phone at the shop. But then your friend Josh showed up out of nowhere and offered to give her a ride home. While they were in his car, he put his hand on her leg and tried to touch her . . . in other places. He told her that he knew she wanted him and that they could be together without telling you. She fought him off, and he wasn't paying attention to the road. The car flipped several times, but ended up in a sandbank, which saved them both from being killed. Zoe took a good lick from the airbag so she's bruised and scratched up. They're running tests to make sure there isn't anything going on internally, but so far it appears that she was damn lucky. They'll keep her overnight for observation as a safety precaution."

Dylan was already on his feet, hell-bent on finding the man who he'd called a friend and brother for all of his adult life. "Where in the hell is that fucker? How dare he put his hands on her? I'll kill him."

Vivian got to her feet and grabbed his hand before he could storm off. "I feel the same way, trust me. But the police are with him. They've already questioned Zoe, and when he's given the all-clear, he'll be going to the station. They're charging him with attempted sexual assault. I want to kick the little weasel's ass just as bad as you do, but my daughter needs us right now, so get your shit together."

Taking a deep breath in an attempt to rein his temper in, he asked, "How is she doing with all this? Shit, I feel like I put this directly on her doorstep, then left her to fend for herself."

"She's in shock, Dylan, which is probably for the best right now. I know you feel guilty, and this may sound bitchy, but right now, this can't be about you. She's been traumatized and she'll need your support and understanding."

He felt like a chastised schoolboy, but she was absolutely right. "When can I see her?"

"I'll go see if she's in a room yet. If you need to make arrangements for work, you should do that now. I know you usually start pretty early each day." He also got her meaning there as well. She was telling him that he'd better not be planning to run out of this hospital anytime soon, which was another dig he deserved.

When she'd walked off, he pulled his phone out and dialed Ash. His brother sounded just as alert at two in the morning as he did at nine. Dylan filled him in briefly on what had happened and held the phone away as Asher cursed colorfully. "Don't worry about anything. I'll make some arrangements. Just take care of your girl."

"Thanks, man," he said gratefully. "I'll touch base with you later on." He sank back down into one of the chairs and dropped his head in his hand. He couldn't believe that Josh had attacked Zoe. He knew he'd been hanging around the shop more, but there had been no indication that it was anything other than friendship. He was so enraged at the thought of him touching his woman that he'd tear him apart limb from limb if he could. Fuck, he'd left her to drive home late at night by herself, while he stayed at the office once again. He'd failed her at every turn and he could have well lost her forever tonight. He had no idea where to go from here, but one thing was certain—something had to change. He could no longer pretend that he could handle everything, because tonight proved that he had let the most important thing in his life become last in line, and that was a bitter pill to swallow.

Nineteen

Zoe muttered a thank-you to Dylan as he brought a blanket over to her sofa and tucked it around her legs. She'd been released an hour earlier and he had driven her home. She'd rebuffed his attempts at conversation since he'd shown up at the hospital shortly after the accident. Truthfully, she was still trying to make sense of everything in her head, so she didn't really know what to say to him. "Would you like something to drink, sweetheart? Maybe some water or coffee?"

Shaking her head, she said softly, "No, nothing right now. I'm just going to rest for a little while. If you need to go to work, I'll be fine."

He looked appalled by her words and she wondered

why. They both knew the Oceanix came first. He sat down on the edge of the sofa next to her and cupped her cheek. "I'm not going anywhere. You're the most important thing to me, and I'll be here until I know that you're okay."

A few days ago, she'd have been thrilled to hear him say that. But now she was confused and unable to think with him watching her every move. She knew it would hurt him, but right now what she wanted more than anything was to be alone. She'd had someone with her since the accident, which meant there had been no time to process what had happened. "Dylan," she began softly, "I really need some space right now. Please don't think I blame you in any way, because I don't. But I could use some time to work everything out on my own. I promise I'll call you, but can you give me that?"

She could see his inner struggle. He wanted to argue. He thought she was angry because Josh was his friend, but that wasn't the case. Right now she didn't have the strength to reassure him further, though. If he didn't leave soon, she was going to crack in front of him, and she very much wanted her privacy for that. "I don't know," he murmured hesitantly. "I'm not sure you should be alone so soon."

Reaching over, she took his hand, saying earnestly, "I need this." With those words, she knew she had him. He might hate it, but he'd never been good at telling her no.

"All right, sweetheart. But promise me you'll check in tonight to let me know you're okay." She nodded her agreement and he bent to drop a kiss on her forehead. "I love you."

"I love you too," she replied. Her love for him had never been the question, but she was starting to realize that possibly it wasn't enough to build a future on, no matter how much she wanted it, unless something changed.

∽

"How's Zoe?" Ash asked as he strolled into the office. Dylan looked up in surprise, having had no idea yet again that he was coming to Florida.

"What are you doing here?" he asked in confusion. When he'd asked his brother to handle things, he hadn't thought it would be in person. After all, he had a hotel to run as well.

"I caught a flight out after I talked to you. I left Hudson in charge of daily operations at the resort. I can handle anything else remotely."

Ash had bragged about his new operations manager, and Dylan had to admit he must be good for his perfectionist brother to turn over the helm to him on such short notice. Hell, maybe he needed to recruit him to come here. "Apparently I spoke too soon anyway because my girlfriend doesn't want me around right now."

"Ouch." Ash whistled before dropping into a seat in front of him. "What's going on? Is she home now?"

"Yeah, I just came from her place. She said she needed some time to think about things." Running a hand through his hair, he admitted, "I feel as if I'm losing her. And the shit thing is, I can't blame her at all. I haven't been there for her. She almost got killed last night because I was here instead of with her. Hell, I didn't even walk her to the car, Ash. It was late when she left and I let her go into the parking garage alone. What kind of man does that?"

"One with far too much on his plate," Ash said. "You're overwhelmed here, and before you think I'm insulting you, hear me out. This location does far more business in a year than the others. You're sitting on a gold mine and it's only going to get bigger. Hence the need for an expansion. I can't believe you made it on your own for this long. None of us could handle all that you do. We've discussed it before. We have no idea how you do it."

"No life and a shitload of antacids," Dylan deadpanned.

"Well, I've got an idea I want to run by you. I think you'll agree that it's in your best interest, so I hope you'll keep an open mind."

"And what will this big plan of yours do for me exactly?" Dylan asked, intrigued despite himself.

Ash sat forward, putting his hands on the edge of

the desk. "It may save your life in more ways than one. Interested?"

"I'm not doing a great job of it on my own, so let's see what you've got." He didn't expect a miracle, but at this point, he certainly didn't have any answers of his own.

Twenty

Zoe was finding out the hard way that avoiding someone who worked in the same building was tricky. Dylan had given her a week, but his calls, texts, and attempts to see her were increasing in frequency and she was almost certain he was watching for her car on the Oceanix surveillance system now. He certainly had a habit of showing up at the coffee shop right after she did. Up until now, she'd managed to always be busy with something, but today she was screwed. The shop had a few people in it, but there was no one at the counter waiting to be served, nor any emergencies she could come up with that she hadn't already used. No, today she was fresh out of ideas and it was time to face the music—or Dylan.

"Good morning." She forced a smile as he took a seat on a stool in front of her.

He studied her carefully as if looking for a clue as to what she was thinking. "Morning, sweetheart. It's good to see you."

"You too," she replied truthfully. Because even as she'd been avoiding him, she'd missed her friend. There was a hole in her life without him that she didn't know quite what to do with.

Running a hand through his hair, he asked, "Will you talk to me now? I know you've been trying to dodge me for days, but I can't take it any longer, sweetheart. I need to know what's going on with you. Hell, I've resorted to bribing half the people at the front desk, the concierge, and the cleaning crew to tell me when you get here every morning. I even groveled to Dana, who told me to do something I'm not sure is even possible with my dick."

Zoe burst out laughing, picturing Dylan lowering his pride for a chance to talk to her. It was a bit of an invasion of her privacy, but the reasoning behind it was sweet. Plus, she hadn't left him much choice. "I don't know what I'm going to do with you and Dana. I'd say you liked each other since you fight so much, but I don't think she has any secret feelings for you."

"Oh, she certainly doesn't," he agreed. "She lets me know exactly what she thinks every time she sees me." They share an amused look before his expression turned serious. "They contacted you about Josh, I heard. I forgot to mention your mother in the list of people I've tried bribing for information on you."

"Yeah," she said softly. "I guess having a rich and powerful daddy helps when you're in trouble."

"He won't be coming anywhere near you again, sweetheart, I promise." For the first time, she noticed his scraped, discolored, and raw knuckles. *Surely he didn't?*

She reached out and picked up one of his hands. He winced slightly, but that was his only reaction. "You went after him, didn't you?"

He turned his hand until their fingers were threaded together. "What else would you have me do? He almost got you killed, Zoe. There was no way I could let that go. He hurt you and betrayed me. His daddy might have gotten him off with community service, but even he was smart enough to stand back and let me at him. He also told me that Josh will be moving back to Chicago with him indefinitely."

"Really?" Zoe asked, sagging with relief at the news. She knew that with him here, she'd always be looking over her shoulder, which was no way to live. "Do you believe him?"

"Actually I do. He's a hard-ass. He won't tolerate something like this happening in his backyard again. He controls the money, so in a sense, he controls Josh through it."

"Thank God," she whispered. "That really gives me some closure."

"Where are we at, baby?" She'd been expecting a similar question, but found she still wasn't prepared for it. Yet she could no longer put this off; he deserved more than that.

"I love you, Dylan. I can't remember a time in my life when I haven't. I once thought that I could handle anything as long as we were together and you felt the same way."

"Why do I sense a 'but' in all of that?" he asked solemnly.

She gave him a sad smile. "You're a very busy man and that's okay. I work a lot of crazy hours too, so I understand that it's necessary sometimes. As much as I love you, I don't want to spend my life waiting for you to come home. I want to get married and have a family one day. But I don't want to do it as a single parent. I was raised by a mother that tried her best to fill both roles for me, but I still felt it when the other kids at school brought their dads to special events and mine wasn't there. I . . . I need something to change, Dylan. I know you have a demanding job, but there has to be a way to have a life outside of the office."

Zoe was surprised when he sat quietly through her entire speech. She'd expected some interruptions or objections, but he'd said nothing. *Wow, doesn't this bother him at all?*

When she was finished, he leaned over the counter and kissed her cheek. "I completely understand what you're saying. Would you agree to have dinner with me tonight? I'll send a car for you. That way, if you want to leave afterward, you won't be dependent on me for a ride home." When she hesitated, he added, "I think we owe each other that much, don't we?"

"All right," she agreed. "I'll be ready at seven if that works for you?"

Getting to his feet, he said, "It's perfect. I'll arrange everything. Thanks for not running from me today." And with that, he was gone and she was something akin to stunned. Or maybe hurt was a more accurate description of what she was feeling. Did he not care what she'd said? Sure, he'd asked to see her tonight, but he'd given no indication that he had any intentions of trying to meet her halfway.

"So what's going on with him?" Dana asked as she walked up to stand next to her.

"I have absolutely no idea," Zoe admitted, "but I think I'm getting a consolation dinner tonight."

"He broke up with you?" the other woman asked in shock.

"No—that's the funny thing. I kind of gave him an ultimatum in a roundabout way. But somehow I feel as if I've played right into his hands. Almost as if there's a plan in place that I don't know about."

"Huh," Dana murmured. "I don't suppose you'd let me come along."

"Um, no," Zoe said, laughing, "not a chance. Although you should probably keep your phone handy in case I need to be talked off a ledge."

"You laid it on the line for him," she pointed out.

"Yeah, but I guess I didn't think he'd seem so unaffected by it."

"He loves you, Zoe. He just needs to realize that while he can. Men are slow sometimes, but I have a feeling he'll get the memo after your little talk today. If not, Mike's still single."

"Oh God," Zoe moaned before turning away. *What have I done?*

❧

Dylan got to his feet as Zoe approached the table. She was stunning in a simple black dress with thin straps that showed off the generous swell of her breasts. *Down, boy. Save it for later. You've got more important matters to take care of first.* "You look beautiful," he said sincerely as he pulled a chair out for her. He'd chosen a local seafood bistro that was one of their favorites. He'd arranged ahead of time to have a secluded table in the corner where they'd have some privacy. Of course, as Ash walked up behind her, he didn't know why that was necessary with his brother along.

"Thank you," she replied as Dylan leaned in to kiss her cheek. *Fuck, I want to taste those lips again.*

"You do look hot," Ash said, causing Zoe to whirl around in shock.

"Asher . . . um, hi. I—I didn't know you were going to be here," she stuttered before shooting Dylan a questioning look.

"He won't be staying for the meal," he assured her. "I just needed him to drop by for a bit to help me out."

She looked confused as to what he'd need assistance with, but she shrugged and took the seat that he indicated. He took his own, leaving the last one for Ash. When Ash took a laptop from the bag he was carrying and set it on the table, Dylan shot him a "what the hell" look. They made small talk until they were relaxing with a bottle of wine. Finally, Zoe said, "All right, this is starting to freak me out. What are we all doing here?"

Before he could answer, Ash laughed and flipped the top on his computer open to show what looked like a PowerPoint presentation. Sure to God he wasn't going to talk work while Dylan was trying to convince Zoe that he'd changed. "I—um, want to talk to you about some new developments that you're unaware of. I'm hoping they'll make a difference to you."

"That's where I come in," Ash interjected. "Instead of us both boring you with a lot of promises, I thought

I'd make it easier to understand." *No, he didn't.* Dylan closed his eyes briefly before glancing at Zoe. She was staring at the screen as if fascinated, which he thought was a good sign. As long as this wasn't some disaster that Ash had made as a joke. The first few screens were basic facts about how the Pensacola location did more business than the others. He had to admit, his brother had skillfully shown why Dylan stayed so busy. He'd also listed all the projects that they had in the works now and in the future.

Shit, now she just looked depressed. This was only confirming her beliefs that he'd never have enough time for her. "Could we get to the point?" He nudged his brother under the table. At this rate, she'd run from the restaurant and never speak to him again before he could get to the best part.

Ash glared at him. He was rather OCD about his presentations and being rushed wasn't something he liked. Thankfully he clicked a few more times and Dylan found himself laughing as a big selfie of his brother filled the screen. *At least he's wearing clothes.* "So yours truly will be moving to Pensacola and dividing the daily responsibilities with Dylan. We've known for a while that the resort is getting too big for one person to handle. My operations manager will take over in Charleston and I'll be here permanently within a month. There will still be some things to work through as we find the right balance, but this should lighten

Dylan's load, allowing him to spend more time with you." With another click, Zoe's image filled the screen with hearts circling her head. *Sweet Lord.*

She threw back her head and laughed before clapping. "That was one of the most informative things I've ever seen. Plus, I now know so much more than I did about the Oceanix."

"I am pretty amazing," Ash bragged. "Oh, wait, I forgot one thing." *Click. No way!* There on the damned screen was a picture of a man on his knees with a diamond extended toward a woman.

While she was gaping at the image, Ash was motioning for him to take action. This was not at all what he'd had in mind for tonight, but the jig was up now. Ash obviously had no intention of leaving before the good part. So Dylan slipped from his seat and almost fell flat on his face before he finally ended up in the correct position. *Click.* Dylan leaned to the side incredulously to see yet another picture, this one instructing her to look down. "I—um, love you so much, Zoe. Will you marry me?" *Real smooth. How could she resist that?*

Tears were running down her cheeks and he had no idea if they were happy or sad ones. Maybe she just felt sorry for him for making a fool out of himself. Then she flew into his arms, knocking him back against the seat as she peppered kisses all over his face. "I can't believe you did all of this for me."

"Technically I did it," Ash inserted before Dylan shot him a look.

"Yes, a thousand times yes! I love you too, Dylan, and I never wanted to be without you. I just couldn't come last anymore. Please say that you understand."

"Of course, sweetheart. I'm ashamed to say that it took almost losing you to make me see that you're more important than anything else in my life. Without you, I can't breathe. You're my one constant and you always have been."

"Oh, Dylan," she cried as he slid the ring on her finger. *Click.* Out of the corner of his eye, he saw the screen change to the words "And they lived happily ever after." For once he had to concede that his brother was indeed a master when it came to presentations. He'd just helped Dylan close the biggest deal of his life.

Epilogue

Zoe stood next to her husband during the ribbon-cutting ceremony for the new addition to the Oceanix Resort. The last year hadn't been easy, but more often than not, Dylan was home for dinner in the evening. Asher had lived up to his word—or his presentation—and had taken a great deal off his brother. Zoe and Dylan had been married three months previous in a quiet ceremony on the beach in front of the resort. She hadn't wanted anything fancy, so it had been only family and a few close friends. Dylan had groaned at the reception when Dana had caught the bouquet. "Some poor bastard has misery coming his way," he'd muttered, then winced when Zoe elbowed him in the side.

"I swear, that man's such an asshole," grumbled her

friend and coworker now as she glared at Asher a few feet away. "When he came in the shop this morning, he told me I needed to stop sampling all the cooking."

Zoe fought back a giggle at Dana's indignant expression. "I'm sure he didn't mean anything by it. You know he has a strange sense of humor sometimes." She was actually quite fond of him now, but it was a woman's duty to side with her friend.

"Oh, really?" Dana huffed. "When I asked, 'What's that supposed to mean?' he said, 'Don't worry about it. Lots of men like women with big butts.'"

Shit. Ash. "You look fine, honey. He's just trying to get a reaction out of you. He picks on me all the time."

"Has he ever called you fat?" she snapped.

"Um . . . well, no," Zoe admitted. "But he didn't exactly say that, did he?"

"Close enough." Luckily Dylan picked that moment to end the conversation he'd been having with someone else.

"What are you two whispering about over here?" he asked as he pulled Zoe back against his chest.

Dana narrowed her eyes and said, "Your brother's a dick. And you're not much better." *There goes the peace.*

Instead of being offended, Dylan laughed. "Yeah, apparently it runs in the family. Why don't you get on your broom and fly back to your castle, where you won't have to deal with it?"

"Dick."

"Witch."

Zoe shook her head before leading her husband away. He enjoyed this verbal sparring far too much. "Will you stop egging her on?" she chided as they walked back inside the resort. "You two are impossible." When he punched in a code on a nearby door and pulled her inside, she looked around in surprise. "Why are we in the janitor's closet?"

He gave her a sexy grin that meant instant wet panties for her. Oh, how she knew that look. "Because you're awfully dirty, Mrs. Jackson, and I believe I have something in here that'll clean you right up."

"Is that so, Mr. Jackson?" Leaning closer to his ear, she palmed his dick and whispered, "First, I'd like to demonstrate my skills with a certain thing I like to call the Hoover." Throaty laughter turned to moans soon after that as she pleasured the first and only man to ever possess her body and soul.

Don't miss

WISHING FOR US

Available now in the Danvers series by Sydney Landon.
Continue reading for a preview.

The relentless pounding in her head was what finally woke Lydia Cross from a sound sleep. Her mouth felt like she had been chewing on a dirty gym sock and her eyes were glued together so tightly it took several attempts for her to pry them open. She lay in a darkened room, attempting to get her bearings. A quick glance at the clock on the bedside table had her sitting up too quickly—which turned out to be a big mistake. Her stomach immediately staged a revolt and she struggled to free herself from under the covers—then promptly smacked into a hard surface. *What the hell?* Who'd moved the wall in her bedroom? She rubbed her smarting nose and inched along with half-closed eyes until she reached a doorway. She fumbled before locating the light switch, then flipped it up. The bright glare that filled the unfamiliar bathroom temporarily blinded her.

After blinking a few times, she was able to focus on her surroundings. Then it finally hit her that she was in Vegas. Her coworker and good friend, Crystal Webber, was getting married to Mark DeSanto in a few days and their friend Mia Gentry had insisted on throwing the bachelorette party at the Oceanix–Las Vegas. Luckily, Danvers was a big company and they were all able to find temporary replacements so they could take a few days of vacation together with no problem.

The nausea that had temporarily abated while she was hunting for the bathroom returned in full force. She barely made it to the toilet before the contents of her stomach came back up in horrifying fashion. She was doing her best to remain upright when her hair was suddenly pulled back and someone touched her back. She jerked in shock, nearly falling into the toilet, before strong hands steadied her. A masculine voice rumbled, "It's okay, little one. I've got you."

Lydia managed to shrug out of the hold long enough to spin around and look at her mystery bathroom guest. "Sweet Jesus," she exclaimed at the sight of Jacob Hay, clad only in snug boxer briefs, towering over her with concern etched on his face. She couldn't help herself—she drank him in from head to toe. Who in the world could possibly blame her for taking advantage of this screwed-up nightmare to check out the man she'd lusted after for months? In all her fantasies, though, she'd never quite imagined him in this scenario. "Wh—what are you doing here?" she asked in confusion, before belatedly realizing that she was also quite nude. She grabbed a robe off a nearby hook and fumbled to put it on.

Jacob raised an amused brow at her. "After last night, I wouldn't have guessed that you had a shy bone in your body, gorgeous."

Oh shit, what's he talking about? Did I wrap myself around him and beg him to come to my room? "You've got three seconds to tell me what in the hell you're doing in my hotel room," she snapped. Thank God, she'd finally gotten the damn robe tied. Laying down the law was rather hard when your boobs were hanging out.

Instead of answering right away, Jacob walked calmly around her and flushed the toilet. He then moved to the sink, unwrapped a toothbrush, and filled a glass with water. He motioned her over and she cringed as she realized he was trying to get her to brush her teeth. Maybe she could pause for a moment to take care of her breath before she continued her inquisition. Lydia quickly took care of business before putting her hands on her hips. "Well?"

He looked as if he was biting back a smile. "Could we possibly take this conversation into the next room?"

She resisted the urge to childishly stomp her feet

as, once again, he made her feel like an idiot. Naturally, he didn't want to stand around and chat in the room she'd just tossed her cookies in. "Oh, all right," she grumbled as she stalked past him. *Wait, I don't remember my room being this nice.*

He moved over to the bedside table and picked up the phone. Despite her glare, he calmly placed an order for coffee and Danishes from room service. Then he turned back to face her. *So hot,* she thought to herself. He studied her for long enough that she began to fidget. When he finally spoke, the deep rumble of his voice in the quiet room had her jerking. "Do you not remember anything about last night?"

Was he nuts? Would she be standing here looking like a complete train wreck if she knew what was going on? But instead of opening her mouth to unleash a sarcastic comment, she took a breath and admitted, "I have no idea. I vaguely remember going dancing at some club with Mia and Crystal." She rubbed her throbbing temple as she attempted to re-create the events of the previous evening. "Didn't Mark and some of his friends show up at some point?"

He had the look of a proud teacher as he nodded his head encouragingly. "That's right. I flew here with Mark and the Jackson brothers. We met up with you ladies sometime during your club crawl."

Images exploded in her head as jumbled memories came rushing back to her. *Dancing. The taste of his lips.*

Our tongues tangling. Hands touching. My new husband. Wait, what? Lydia stared at Jacob in dawning horror before looking down at the glittering diamond on her ring finger.

Holy. Fucking. Shit.

"We got married," she whispered, then promptly staggered over to the bed and dropped down onto it.

Acknowledgments

As always, a special note of thanks to my agent, Jane Dystel, and my editor at Penguin, Kerry Donovan. None of this would ever be possible without you both, and I appreciate all that you do.

To my special friends: Amanda Lanclos and Heather Waterman from Crazy Cajun Book Addicts, Catherine Crook from A Reader Lives a 1000 Lives, Shelly Lazar from Sexy Bibliophiles, Christine with Books and Beyond Fifty Shades, Marion Archer, Lorie Gullian, Stacia from Three Girls and A Book Obsession, Shannon with Cocktails and Books, Sarah from Smut and Bon Bons, Andrea from The Bookish Babe, Jennifer from Book Bitches Blog, Tracey Quintin, Melissa Lemons, Lisa Granger, Chantel Pentz McKinley, Nicole Tallman, Stefanie Eldrige-O'Toole, Tara Thomas, Lisa Salvary, Monique Harrell-Watford, Kim Roar, Sandy Ambrose, and Jen Maxner.

Sydney Landon is the *New York Times* and *USA Today* bestselling author of the Danvers Novels, including *Watch Over Me* and *The One for Me*. She lives in South Carolina with her husband and two children, who keep her life interesting and borderline insane, but never boring. When she isn't writing, Sydney enjoys reading, swimming, and being a minivan-driving soccer mom.

NEW YORK TIMES BESTSELLING AUTHOR
SYDNEY LANDON

Find more books by Sydney Landon
by visiting prh.com/nextread

PRAISE FOR THE NOVELS OF SYDNEY LANDON

"Wonderful . . . . Landon's foray into contemporary
romance has just the right amount of angst, sass,
sexiness, humor, and, of course, romance."
—Fresh Fiction

"Enough bittersweet longing to pluck your
heartstrings and enough heat to keep it interesting."
—*Kirkus Reviews*

sydneylandon.com
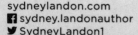 sydney.landonauthor
SydneyLandon1